THE WALLED GARDEN

THE WALLED GARDEN

*A Romance of the
Jazz Age*

ROWAN MAI

Bergamot Press

Contents

Part I: A Most Rare Vision

I have had a most rare vision. I have had a dream—past the wit of man to say what dream it was. Man is but an ass if he go about to expound this dream. Methought I was—there is no man can tell what. Methought I was, and methought I had— but man is but a patched fool if he will offer to say what me- thought I had. The eye of man hath not heard, the ear of man hath not seen, man's hand is not able to taste, his tongue to conceive, nor his heart to report what my dream was.

— Bottom, *A Midsummer Night's Dream*, William Shakespeare

The noise of the party diminished the farther she persisted in her wandering, which was of course her aim; by the time she reached the east wing, the babble of the guests and the frantic band had entirely abated. She felt a vicious jab of pleasure upon achieving her goal. This subsided into the simpler satisfaction of snooping at her leisure, buoyed up by the effects of several glasses of champagne.

Some hours earlier, the east wing had been described to her by the host—the coal magnate—as "the Tudor Hall." Now she gazed, not unimpressed, at soaring oak-paneled walls, a series of tapestries depicting a hunt, and hulking carven chairs that looked as if they had previously housed bishops awaiting their beheadings. She sipped her champagne; she walked on. It had all been constructed less than twenty years ago, of course, but the effect was total. Even the electric lighting was tastefully low. She allowed herself a sense of reverie: she might have been a time-traveler. On an impulse, she called out ringingly to the woven hunters on the wall: "Tantivy, tantivy!"—and raised her glass in toast to them. The half-full bottle of champagne with which she'd absconded was a happy weight in her other hand, and she swung it loosely as she walked on.

At the far end of the hall, a Gothic archway gave onto to the darkness of what looked like a games room, where billiard tables lurked under padded leather coverings, like staunch, blanketed horses. She found herself restraining laughter at the self-conscious masculinity of it all. To the left of the archway, a small, enclosed half-flight of stairs disappeared into darkness, carpeted thickly with the same leafy motif as the hunt tapestries.

Along the wall at the left of the foot of the stairs there was an array of large and imposingly dour portraits in gilt frames. She lifted her champagne glass and rested it against her lower lip, not drinking, as she scanned the gallery of fat-faced dukes in furs and hollow-eyed women whose pasty fingers looked pinched off by stacks of gold rings. What had they been thinking about as they had had their portraits painted? Lunch, probably. A sick child. An annoying mother-in-law...

"He imported the aristocratic relations, of course," someone said suddenly, "just like the rest of the décor in the hall."

She started, disoriented, and looked around. A light had appeared at the top of the little staircase: how long had she been staring at the portraits, drifting? Silhouetted against the light was a figure—a man—sitting at the top of the stairs, slightly hunched.

She stared, wordless, rankled. She'd been caught unawares, and resented it, resented the interruption of her private reverie. She felt the return of the vicious mood that had driven her away from the party in the first place.

"Have I scared you? I beg your pardon," said the figure.

"I'm not scared," she said loudly and sharply. "You don't have to beg."

The figure laughed. The laugh sounded odd, perhaps nervous, and then it—he—moved in a way that was also odd, a sort of lurch to one side, his head rolling to that shoulder also.

"Oh good," he said, "then maybe I won't have to do much to convince you to share some of that champagne with me."

Slowly she turned away from the portrait gallery and took a few steps closer to the staircase, squinting upward. "So those aren't his great-grand-whatevers, then?" she said, evading his suggestion. "Not even distantly?"

After a moment, he laughed again. "Not even distantly. The Byrnes are Irish through and through. Upstarts in American soil." Despite her irritation, it struck her that his voice was delicious: it had a kind of easeful theatricality, deliberation balanced by humor.

She wished the light were better; she tried to examine him more closely. He was not much older than her, she thought, but so lean, even thin, that it made him look older, especially in the dim lighting, which cast heavy shadows under his cheek-bones. He had dark, slightly waving hair, deeply parted on one side and cut rather short. His nose was pronounced, balanced by a wide mouth. From what she could see, his eyes were deep-set, narrow, in a way that accentuated the sense of habitual humor that he gave off. He was wearing a crisp shirt and tie, but no vest or jacket.

Under her gaze, he moved again, and the movement was undeniably unnatural, a kind of rolling spasm that seemed to travel the length of his whole body, stretching some joints and collapsing others. She noticed that, leaning towards her, he had hung his arms straight down between his bent knees, and was gripping one wrist with the other hand; both hands jerked gently.

She raised the bottle of champagne and put her head to one side. "Are you sure you haven't had enough already?"

He paused. "Would you believe me," he said, "if I said I hadn't had a drop all evening? Maybe that's what's the matter with me. If you *do* share and it turns out your champagne has cured a lifelong affliction, I'll be awfully in your debt."

She kept looking at him, uncertain. She thought that a note of strain had entered that lilting voice, but it was hard to say.

"Damn," he said finally. "You're not really drunk, are you?" His body moved restlessly.

She didn't bother answering, just kept looking.

"I'm a cripple, you see," he said, as if in response to something she had said. His voice had not risen at all, but its gaiety had become cutting.

The questions that had been turning slowly in her mind stopped, clicking together. A new rank rose to take their place.

"Who are you?" she asked curiously, taking another step forward.

He answered with another question: "Have you met Winston Byrne?"

"Winston? The middle brother? The one who's mad about horses—polo and things?"

"That one. The centaur."

She smiled uncertainly; she waited for him to say something else. When he didn't, she turned over the image of Winston in her head, looking for a clue. Though the youngest Byrne son was fair and rounded, like their mother, the elder two took after their father. Winston in particular was dark, tall, very upright, sunburnt brown, edgy and superior. He always looked as if he were wanting a riding crop he could whack into his thigh in order to more fully express himself. She felt bad for the women who trailed after him because she could sympathize; there was something mindlessly attractive about the hard-edged masculinity that he exuded.

She thought about his lean, rawboned frame; his prominent, somewhat knobbed nose and sun-weathered cheekbones. She began to get an uncomfortable feeling. Take Winston Byrne: take away the sun, the hard-packed muscle...

"You," she began to say to the man on the stairs, taking another step forward, squinting again.

"I think you begin to see," he said. "Well, nobody would have told you he had a twin brother."

"*Twin* brother," she breathed. She felt it like a shock of cold water. She had only gotten as far as maybe a cousin, *maybe* a brother—

"It's unfortunate, isn't it," he said, almost apologetically. Another of those spasms ran through him: one of his feet kicked out abruptly and dropped down one step, and one of his arms gestured oddly. Trying to interpret it, she realized that he had lost his grip on the wrist of that arm, so it was now wandering through the air by itself.

"Well," she said, and stopped, unsure of how to continue, trying not to watch him trying to recapture his own arm.

"What's your surname?" he said, helpfully filling in the silence. After several awkward grabbing motions, he had resettled his grip on his wrist; his hands sank between his legs again.

"De Vries," she said softly.

"Miss De Vries," he said.

"Helena," she added automatically.

"Helena De Vries," he said thoughtfully. "Of the Philadelphia De Vries?"

"Those ones," she said.

"Hmm. Michael Byrne, at your service. You see," he said, as if continuing an earlier train of thought, "it's not too uncommon for twins—especially the younger—to be afflicted with palsy, after a difficult birth. You're about to spill."

Hastily she looked down and righted her glass just as she was about to let it list too far to one side. "Thank you," she said uncertainly. She found that her cheeks were hot.

There was a laden pause. Having looked away, she kept her gaze slightly averted from him. Finally he said, "You haven't met someone like me before, I suppose." How could he keep talking so lightly? But she could hear the effort it cost him, too.

"No," she admitted. Certainly she had seen them in city streets before—poor children, ragged weary men on crutches —or in blurry newspaper images of veterans from the Great War, but she wouldn't say that out loud.

"Well," he said, "I did hear you crying the hunt, and thought I might come see what game was afoot, if you'll pardon the expression. But I've disturbed you, when you took the trouble to come be by yourself here in the first place. I can retire, and leave you to enjoy your evening."

"Do they make you stay back there?" she said, raising her eyes to look at him again. Her spirits had gathered again, into something like anger. "In—what—the servants' quarters?"

"They're *my* quarters," he said, "but, yes, it's much the same idea. Wouldn't you do the same thing if you had a son like me?" With a wrenching gesture, he lifted both his hands, to show her their trembling. After a few moments, they dropped back down again heavily, as if he didn't have the strength to keep them raised.

"Don't be cruel," she said, deeply stung. "How could you say something like that when I've just been talking with you? And seen—"

He waited for her to complete her thought, but she found she couldn't express what she meant.

"So what you're saying," he said then, "is that champagne is not entirely out of the question."

She laughed, and the feeling was lovely. Without another word, she went up the stairs to him. When she reached his level, she stopped and, with deliberation, topped off the champagne glass. She could feel his eyes on her as she poured; the hiss of the bubbles that sprang up in the glass sounded dangerously loud in the waiting silence. She bent and deposited the bottle on the landing above. She turned back to him, beginning to outstretch the glass, and then hesitated. "Do you need...?"

"Yes. Please."

She sat next to him and stretched out the glass to his lips. A moment later, seeing how he struggled to keep his head still, she put her other hand to the back of his head, gently steadying it.

"Thank you," he murmured, flicking his eyes up to hers. He held her gaze for a moment. Then she tipped the glass, and he drank.

After a few swallows, abruptly his head fell to one side, and she failed to catch it in time, so a little champagne spilled on the corner of his mouth. Swiftly she withdrew the glass, murmuring in dismay. He righted his head, grimacing. Without thinking, she put her finger to the corner of his mouth and let her black satin glove soak up the little trickle of champagne.

He looked at her. His eyes were very dark. Hastily she withdrew her hand, dropped her gaze.

They turned and looked out over the dim hall. She held the glass of champagne a little stiffly, as if it were no longer hers. She listened to the rustling as his body moved restlessly. She discerned a strange sense of guilt in herself: as if she had seen something she shouldn't have—or even as if she were personally responsible for his condition. How could that be? Perhaps she ought to leave, anyway... But there was a pull, there, in that dimly lit, antiquated hall, where it could have been any century and any hour of the night. She wanted to stay there; she wanted to hear more, somehow get ahold of a sense of reality of this strange man.

It struck her, also, that she couldn't remember the last time she had sat and really enjoyed the conversation of a man.

She drank from the glass again. "So," she said, "appropriated ancestry. A secret scion in the east wing. Please tell me, does your..." She hesitated; it was still hard to believe. "Does your father also have a literal skeleton in a closet somewhere? A suspicious tibia, at least?"

He laughed. "I don't know if he has the imagination for anything so exciting. If there's a forbidden vault somewhere in the house, it probably just has stacks of bonds and deeds inside. Then again, I did used to like to imagine him being quite the adventurer when he was a young surveyor. People do like to exclaim over how much Winston brings back the younger Father."

And where did that leave him, she thought, who was Winston's twin? She pushed the thought away. "Did you imagine him—what, murdering a claim-jumper? Swimming a flooded river to deliver an urgent message? Fending off an enraged mother bear?"

He laughed. "All of those, and more. And then the next time I saw him, I'd see him complaining about the texture of the boiled potatoes or whatever, and think, my god, he'd probably just lecture the bear about land lease agreements until she stumbled away to drown herself."

"But anyway," he continued, as she smiled to herself, "what brought you out here, to our West Coast?" Out of the corner of her eye, she saw his body lurch, and she realized that he had turned to look at her, but his body's awkwardness had forced his head to twist at a strange angle, while one of his shoulders had dropped forward.

She shifted; she found that her cheeks had warmed again. "I'm helping my aunt with her archives."

"Archives?" His voice had brightened with curiosity.

"She's a sort of—she traveled the world a great deal when she was young, and she has all sorts of letters and maps and things. And art—lots of it."

"And does she have good taste?"

"She has excellent taste."

"Oh, thank god." As she laughed, he said, "I just can't imagine having to sort through stacks of lifeless paintings while numbly agreeing with auntie that yes, it's all remarkable."

"No, no, she's not that kind of aunt," she said quickly. At the same time, she thought that, for the first time, something about his urbanity had grated on her. She paused briefly to fish out the notion: he was forcing it, it was too clear that he was putting it on, this appearance that he had met and passed judgement on lots of people and things. Well, what did she know about his life, really? Maybe he had. But no—the slightly too-forceful artfulness with which he acted that experience was its own giveaway.

But again, she pushed those thoughts away.

"She's really an original," she resumed, "she traveled all over —Morocco, Egypt, India—and she refused to ever get married. Her taste is—it's surprising, in little ways. She likes beauty, of course—anything that's too modern repels her—but she doesn't mind things that are broken, or stained. She has a way of picking things so that it seems like part of the piece. She likes silver better when it's tarnished..."

She could sense him smiling beside her. "That sounds lovely.

I'd like to see some of her collection... And so you're here for—what, one month? To help?"

"I'm here for the summer. And maybe again in the winter, if some plans work out. She's hoping to start a little museum, you see, with her collection," she finished, a little bashfully.

"Why do you say that as if you're embarrassed?"

"Oh," she said, startled. "I... well, it's something I really want to happen, and I suppose I feel that it's my project, too, and... I don't know. Maybe I'm a little superstitious about things that aren't entirely worked out yet."

He gave a speculative *hmm.*

She straightened and was about to offer him more champagne to cover her embarrassment, but then put her hand out and touched his arm. "Hold on—"

He jerked. "What is it?"

Coming towards them, distant at first but growing with great speed, was a stream of confused laughter. Two voices, a man's and a woman's, very drunk—she could hear them careening and stumbling, alternating giddy laughter with exaggerated shushing. They arrived at the archway to the Tudor Hall with a particularly shrill burst of laughter from the man. She felt Michael jerk under her hand again, this time slipping out from under her touch. She froze, as the woman at the other end of the hall cried out, "Oh!"

"What is it? What's it?" the man slurred. She could see him slumping against the doorway; the woman glimmered in a short silver dress.

"It's spooky in there," the woman cried.

"Oh? Ghosts?"

"No, don't say that—"

"I'm sure there are ghosts," the man said leeringly. "Here comes one now—ooooo..."

And they veered back in the opposite direction, shrieking.

Helena let out a breath. She looked to Michael, about to make a jesting remark, but found, to her dismay, that he had collapsed across the steps, his limbs sprawled out in every direction. His back was arched awkwardly to one side, his head had been forced back, and his lips were pressed together into a tight grimace. The fingers of his upraised right arm twitched in and out of a claw.

Her gaze flickered across his form rapidly in distress. Should she try to help him? What if she hurt him? Was it some kind of fit? —no, she could see that his eyes were focused, and hear that his breath was regular, if harsh with exertion. His eyes met hers briefly, and then flicked away deliberately.

"Mr. Byrne?" she whispered. "Are you all right? Can I help you?"

He grunted and then shook his head a fraction of an inch. She could hear and see that he was trying to force deeper breaths; his ribcage swelled against his shirt.

She continued watching for any signal that she should help. A few moments later, he forced his head back into a more natural position, and said faintly, "I'll be another minute." His eyebrows were drawn together severely, she wasn't sure if with frustration, discomfort, or both. Slowly he drew his feet back together, one at a time, and then with his better arm, the left one, pushed himself back up to sitting. His right arm had twisted into another strange configuration, raised and sharply bent, with his hand pressing into his own neck, but he appeared to have given up on it for now.

"Don't look so stricken," he said, smiling wanly at her. His speech sounded a little thick. "This is just how things are. You are remarkably patient, though."

During that spell, she had for the first time allowed herself to wonder what it would be like to not be able to trust any part of your body, to be bound to such an uncertain vehicle. He spoke of patience: surely his life required nothing but that. She wondered what it was like for him to see his twin brother striding around, racing off to drive, play with his horses, court women... But then again, how often would he really have seen his brother at all—or any of his family? If he was more or less confined to his own quarters—and she doubted any of his brothers was the type to stop by for a confiding chat...

He must have seen something of these thoughts in her expression because he said then, "Please don't pity me. I find it encourages bad habits in me."

Abashed, she looked aside. She found she had set down the champagne glass at some point in the confusion with their drunken guests; she extended it to him again, a peace offering, and he accepted gratefully, this time drinking without mishap.

"It was as if they came at us out of another century," she said, looking out again at the hall when he had finished. The tips of her gloved fingers felt warm, where she had supported his head.

"There's a dreamy thought. I wouldn't have minded a century with less drunken shrieking."

"Has there been one without any?"

"A fair question. We might have to look back to somewhere circa Eden... I do keep hoping that some interesting ghosts might find themselves drawn here out of sympathy with the décor, but no luck yet. If our visitants were from the past, at least we might hope to learn some things from them."

"You should ask your father to ensure that the next round of imported portraiture comes with at least one respectable ghost attached."

"If my father ever spoke to me, I would. *You* should ask your aunt."

"She does have a Mughal dagger that is supposed to be cursed."

"Oh?"

"There's a blackened fingerprint on the blade—no matter how many times you clean it, it always comes back in a day or so. There's a whole story about it, with a usurper and a faithless bride, of course."

"Oh—I would like to see that. Maybe one day I'll be able to go to your aunt's museum, and you'll be there sitting in a little office where you'll give me a ticket. You'll take me inside and tell me all the stories about usurpers you can manage."

She smiled down at her interlaced fingers. "Maybe."

"Would you like to see *my* museum?"

"Excuse me?"

He craned his head back over his shoulder to indicate the

little passageway turning off from the stairs. "Where I live. Would you like to see it?"

She hesitated. His dark eyes glinted at her hopefully, and he swayed slightly where he sat, with his arms once again hanging between his knees, left hand tightly clasped around right wrist. Part of her said that it was getting later and later, that this entire exchange was ill-advised for any number of reasons, and that she ought to take this moment to excuse herself; but it was a small, dry voice. The rest of her didn't even have words; it simply wanted to see where the night would keep going.

"I would like to see that, yes," she said, and was rewarded with the sight of his face creasing with a deeply warm smile.

She was startled when he pushed himself up the stairs without another word, using his legs alone, and then set off down the hallway in the same fashion, pushing himself backwards with short, deliberate thrusts of his legs. She rose and turned to follow him down the oak-paneled hallway. A little way down the passage, she saw a high-backed wheelchair of wood and wicker, backed against one wall.

The sight gave her a pang: that weighty image of infirmity, confinement. Until she had seen the wheelchair, it was as if Michael had simply been his own type of creature, with his own curious ways of doing things. The wheelchair reminded her that... what?

That he was a man who needed a wheelchair, and had been placed in quarters that terminated in stairs.

Michael positioned himself in front of the chair and then

turned to her with a measuring look. "My chariot awaits. Won't you help me up, my dear Hippolyta?"

She hesitated, discomfited. He said hurriedly, "It won't take much strength from you, just balance. I know this is an imposition, but to be frank, it will be much less—ugly than if I try by myself."

Helena went to him, more than a little trepidatious, but moved by his expression of pride.

"You'll need to put your hands under my arms," he said, "yes, like that—and then rise when I rise. You won't need to take my weight for more than a moment. Ready? Good—I'm going—"

He pressed himself upwards. His legs shook constantly, and his arms twisted loosely at his sides, but it was true that he was able to take his full weight on his feet. It was simply that he had no balance whatsoever, she realized: her hands were there to keep him from pulling himself off center, to push back when his torso jerked to one side. Like this, she was able to help him into his chair with fair speed.

"Thank you," he said as he settled himself. His eyes sought hers, but she glanced back deliberately over her shoulder. "That bottle..." she said, and turned back to retrieve it. Behind her, she could hear a small squeak from one wheel as he set off down the hallway.

She came up behind him as he exited the hallway into a long, high-ceilinged gallery: somewhat narrow, but wonderfully lofty. The left-hand wall was lined with bookshelves, while the right was a rank of mullioned windows stretching almost the entire height of the wall, showing the blue-black night. The bookshelves were untidily filled to about the height of Michael's head; a few curious objects were scattered among the higher shelves. A low, round, heavy table sat in the far corner of the gallery, against the windows, and was overspread with more books, most of them open.

She found that she was smiling. Michael had come to a stop a little way ahead of her. She realized belatedly that he did not use his unruly hands to propel the wheels of his chair; rather, he pulled himself along with his feet. Now, he used one foot to push the chair around until he faced her again.

"It must be lovely in the daytime," she said, "with all the light.

"It is." There was a note of pride in his voice.

She walked closer to one of the windows, peering through the reflection of the lights. Outside she could see a stone parapet and the darkness of the grounds below. The parapet was ornamental, she realized; there was no balcony outside. Had someone, she wondered, been determined that there be no chance for the occupant of this gallery to be visible from the outside?

She turned back; Michael had made his way to the table and was looking at one of the books there, his head slowly twisting on his neck with that characteristic motion. She went to join him, setting down the champagne bottle off to one side. "*The Decameron*," he said brightly to her, "always good company."

She gazed down. "Yes, plague stories," she said absently, "stories to divert..."

"The confined," he suggested helpfully.

She refrained from responding. The copy was open to the story of Martellino, and looked very old – leather-bound, with heavy, brown-edged pages. It showed signs of rough handling, with pages crumpled or even hanging askew. The same was true of all the other books piled on the table; she thought of his shaking hands. Slowly she ran one of her own fingers over the spines of a haphazard stack.

"Mr. Byrne," she said carefully. He looked at her quizzically. "I have an impertinent question."

"Well, you've roused my curiosity. What is it?"

"Isn't it... unkind," she said, "for your family to... keep you alone, and at the top of a flight of stairs?"

He rocked back in his chair and looked at her. An expression of something like contempt flickered over his face, only for an instant, but seeing it, she felt a sharp twist of emotion in her stomach: regret, shame, a defensive thrust of her own pride. She forced herself to look at him squarely, following the motions of his unsteady head, examining his sharp eyes, the lines on either side of his mouth.

"Miss De Vries," he said finally, "you mean well, I'm sure, but are you aware that the most likely alternative would be my placement in an institution?"

Her stomach sank. "I'm sorry," she said very softly, barely able to hold his gaze now. "I should have thought."

"Perhaps you should have. Even so, I imagine you wouldn't be aware," he continued inexorably, "that California has, very recently, approved a succession of laws allowing the sterilization of many inhabitants of such institutions. For the future betterment of the human race. I don't think my own mother even knows that I know that."

She stared away to one side, silent. Her face had gone utterly cold. She felt her skin creeping with slow horror.

"My parents took a sizable risk," he continued coolly, "in choosing to care for me at home. For years they had no idea whether I would be able to think, or walk, or speak. Obviously some of those things turned out better than others. Nonetheless. Neither my father nor my mother are sentimental people. We can speculate as to their reasons for keeping me at home; I certainly have. We might conclude it was pride more than anything else, pride in their wealth. Still, I must choose to feel gratitude for my circumstances. For my *considerable* advantages. Anything else would drive me mad."

She could feel his gaze on her, heavily; she lifted her face to meet it. "I'm sorry," she said again, "for my presumptuousness." She felt very young.

"Well, anyway," he said, with that studied lightness she had detected before, jerking his arms about in his lap as if to clear the air, "I'm not so very alone here. The servants are wonderful gossips. And Mother comes to see me every day. And Lewis more frequently than you might expect." That was the youngest brother; it *was* a pleasant surprise to hear.

"You're still thinking a great many thoughts—rebellious thoughts," he remarked, with something like the contemptuous look he had revealed before, but affectionate this time. His head was listing to one side, giving him an incidentally rakish look. "You're thinking, for example, that my family ought to be more courageous about my situation; to not treat me as something to be ashamed of; to use their position to force better treatment... *Et cetera*. How old are you, Miss De Vries?"

"You don't need to rub it in," she said evenly. "But I'm twenty-two."

"That makes me," he said, "more than ten years older than you are," and she tried not to show her surprise. "I've had all that time, and more, to think the same thoughts that you are right now. At present, I find it more restful not to take up that train anymore."

She could find nothing to say, then. She continued watching him, his body's restless involuntary rearrangements, the way the fingers of his right hand trembled open and closed around nothing. She had a sudden notion of being in a garden on a cold spring day, of watching the wind push a flower's petals open and then shut again.

He gave her that affectionate look again; this time it was less edged. "And what are you thinking now?"

"Do you remember you asked me," she said slowly, "why I was embarrassed to talk about my aunt's museum?"

"Yes," he said curiously.

"I was embarrassed," she said, running her hand back and forth along the edge of the book-laden table, "because ever since I was twelve, I've had a fear that I wasn't real. I wasn't real, none of the words I said, nothing I did was real. Before you give me another of your looks—I know I wasn't exceptional for feeling that way. But the feeling *was* very real to me, if that isn't a paradox. I started to look around me for people who seemed to be real, so they could show me how. Pretty soon I realized there were precious few. My aunt was one of them, of course. But she was so *very* her own person that I couldn't see my own way to being that way, myself. I thought that I could only end up *like* that—acting like her, if you see what I mean.

"Still, the more I worked with her... the more I work with her, the more we plan, the more I have the sense that this could be the *first* real thing that I do, this making a museum. Making a place where people can go and see beauty, see things they haven't seen before, and think about places they haven't been before, and the people who live there... A place where people can be still." She shrugged. "Probably it's silly, but it's what I've been thinking, more and more. Isn't it dreadful what being rich does to one's character? Or at least mine." She tried to put on a careless smile, but faltered when she saw how genuinely he was, in fact, smiling at her just then.

She forced herself onward. "Anyway, I've gone on about all of this in order to explain: I'm confident that you're the only real person I've met this whole time, since coming west. And I truly am sorry for my thoughtlessness about... your situation. It's just hard... meeting you, and then not wanting better for you."

"Why," he said, very softly, "thank you."

In the silence that followed, she crossed the few steps that separated them. She reached out to take his hands; at her touch, his left hand unclenched its grip around his right wrist, so that she could take each hand separately. It hadn't been deliberate, she realized in another moment: once again his whole body was thrusting itself into a strange posture, as when he had been startled by the drunken revelers, back in the hall. His hands jerked roughly at her grasp as his shoulders wrenched to one side, and she could hear his breath coming quickly. His eyes had widened with dismay, and his cheeks were flushed. But she held on tightly, feeling the warmth of his hands through her gloves, and their wiry, uncoordinated strength.

Gradually his body quieted, slackened. He looked up at her disbelievingly. She leaned in closer. "Would you like to...?" she said quietly.

"Yes," he said, and she bent down to kiss him.

He breathed out tremblingly when they parted. His eyes flickered back and forth over her face, so bright that they looked liquid. Again she could hear his breath coming fast. Gently she released his hands, trying to lay them to rest in his lap.

In the ordinary course of things, she would have liked nothing better now than to sit with him, to mingle touching and kissing and soft talk, to try to explain to him with her presence and her gestures how open and how safe he made her feel at the same time.

But the cozy gallery felt suddenly exposed, its ceilings too high and windows too large. She imagined a sharp-eyed gardener peering through the foliage below, or the sudden arrival of a maid dispatched to bring Michael leftover canapés from the party.

And there was no "ordinary course," here. Her mind flooded with questions she hadn't dared to entertain before: had he ever kissed a woman before—or more? How often did he even speak with women who weren't his mother, a maid, or a house-keeper? She remembered how superior she had felt when she had first detected his put-upon air of worldliness; she felt the unkindness of that now... Was it possible for a *woman* to take advantage of a man?

Her thoughts were scattering every which way, running away into wordless uncertainty. She couldn't look him in the eye.

In the end, the thing that brought her back was the memory of her own words: *This could be the first real thing that I do.* She thought of the strangeness of this night, its dreamlike, vivid quality of possibility, which had peeled back the numbness and irony that had become habitual to her. She thought of the strangeness of the man, of Michael Byrne's beautiful voice and smile and his singular, willful body.

What is real, she thought, *is how I felt when I kissed him. And how I felt when he looked at me afterward.*

"Mr. Byrne," she said abruptly.

His head rocked back. "That is my name, yes," he said, and she had to laugh.

"I find that I am feeling faint," she said, and found that she was appropriately breathless. "Would you do me the favor of bringing me somewhere quieter—more private—so that I might recover myself?"

Again he started, his arms striking out and falling to one

side in his lap. When he had examined her face and found that she was entirely serious in what she was suggesting, his eyes widened.

His voice was grave when he spoke. "You do look pale, Miss De Vries. It would be my pleasure to convey you to more private quarters."

He put one foot out to begin to push himself away from the table. Then he bit out half of an exclamation as his body buckled in on itself, his torso collapsing down and to one side, one of his knees lifting sharply off the ground.

"God!" he said sharply when he was able to unfold himself again. His face was tense with anger. "You had better push me," he said to her, "unless you are, reasonably, having second thoughts about... all of this."

In answer, she moved around to put her hands on the push-bar at the back of his chair and began wheeling him out of the gallery. Beyond, there was a short passageway, which opened out again into a smaller, square room filled with a startling profusion of potted plants; briefly, delightedly, she perceived that in one corner there stood a tall cage with a few small birds sleeping inside. Beyond that there was another passageway, ending in an open door; to their left there was another door, closed. "The one ahead?" she asked him, bending to whisper directly into his ear.

"Yes," he said; his voice still sounded thick, as if he were forcing it out. His head was lolling towards his chest; she pushed him onward.

The room was large and noticeably warm, and a four-poster

bed commanded the left-hand wall. The thrill of taboo possessed her: to be in a man's bedroom, alone...

To one corner stood a twin of the round table in the gallery, with only slightly fewer books on it. Along the wall opposite the bed was a low dresser bearing a broad tray packed with medicine-bottles, and a basket holding an assortment of what looked like leather bands or straps and metal instruments. She felt his discomfort as soon as he saw her noticing those, and turned her gaze away again swiftly. She moved to close the door; to her surprise there was a key in the lock on the inside. She turned it with both satisfaction and something close to fear. She turned to see him looking up at her from his wheelchair with a strikingly similar expression.

"Here we are," she breathed. At first slowly, and then with growing impatience, she stripped her long black gloves from each hand and dropped them to one side. Again she stepped forward and reached for him, but this time she moved to cup his face. Her hands might have been trembling. She felt the jolt of reaction run through him; his eyes closed as the tremors traveled his body. Slowly she ran her fingers over his face, feeling the pleasant scrape of stubble, tracing the lines on either side of his mouth, the contours of his parted lips. Yes, her hands were trembling. Both their breaths were coming fast. She bent to kiss him again and again.

When she opened her eyes again, she was amazed to see tears standing in his eyes. "Don't do that," she said, laughing out of alarm or embarrassment. She reached out with her thumbs and quickly wiped the tears away; then let one of her thumbs slide down again to rest by the corner of his lovely wide mouth.

"Sorry," he said, "I'll try not to." He was laughing too, caught up in the same absurd emotional state. His head dropped to one side, his shoulders slumping. "What shall we do about all this?" he said, more softly, gesturing vaguely with his linked arms.

She couldn't think through everything his question could have meant. She answered with willful ambiguity: "In a moment, I'll help you... But will you move to the foot of your bed?" Watching her curiously, he did, pulling himself forward in his chair. At the same time, she moved to the opposite wall, before the dresser, taking deliberate, backward steps. She paused before the dresser, smoothing her hands over the fabric at her hips. Then she twisted and began to undo, one by one, the side closures of her gown, the long, fitted column of finely pleated black silk with crystals at the bodice. She pretended to ignore him watching her, the sheer weight of his gaze on her, the constant rustling and occasional creak of the wooden chair as his body shifted.

She slipped the gown off her shoulders, let it slither heavily to the floor, enjoying the cool passage of the fabric. She heard him let out a long breath. She stood in her black slip, her sheer stockings. She allowed herself to look up at him again, waiting there across the room. The desire in his eyes was so bright and fierce that she almost took a step back, but she held herself, poised, looking back at him almost challengingly. His body convulsed; his right hand groped helplessly, trying to escape from the grasp of his other hand.

Swiftly she went to him then. She knelt and reached out to undo his tie, his shirt, pretending, with a strange secret pleasure, to ignore it as his linked hands brushed or pushed with a kind of desperate randomness across her face, her neck, her shoulders—except that once she lowered her head to kiss his knuckles in passing. She heard his sharp intake of breath.

"Let go," she said eventually, tugging gently at his hands. When he released his clasp, she pulled him forward slightly so that she could guide each of his arms out of its sleeve, pull the shirt away.

He was so thin, hardly more than bone and muscle. Fine dark curling hair ran down his chest; she ran her hand down to the place where the line disappeared into the waistband of his trousers, then ran it back up, watching with a strange mixture of satisfaction and dismay as he convulsed again in reaction, his head straining back, the cords in his neck standing out. "Is this all right?" she whispered hastily.

He forced his head back up. "Yes. Yes." She could see sweat on his brow.

"It doesn't hurt you—when your body moves like that?"

"Only sometimes. Rarely."

She wasn't sure whether to believe him, but was distracted when he abruptly brought his arms down on either side of his face, fumbling until he could once again link his arms together, so that he was, in his way, holding her. Like this, he pulled her closer to him. She was smiling broadly with delight. It was all strange, so strange, and yet so intimate, almost unbearably so; it was like nothing she had ever known before. This time, he kissed her, rough, clumsy, urgent.

He leaned back again. His eyes were searching her face almost frantically, as if waiting for a reaction that was not forthcoming. His arms were warm on her shoulders. "How can you want me?" he said finally, his voice breaking. "How can you?"

She reached up and took his face again. "I already told you," she said softly. Then she reached back and drew his arms over her head again so that she could grasp each of his curled, trembling hands before her and, with them, stroke her cheeks, her neck, run them down her waist... She slid one inside her black slip to stroke around one of her breasts—he moaned, and the sound stirred her deeply. She left the hand there for another moment, then drew it out, clasped the two hands together again so that he could steady himself. "Let's go," she said, smiling.

He grinned back at her in answer, his eyes glinting. With his feet he pulled his chair to one corner of the bed, where he wrapped his arms around the bedpost, and then, to her great surprise, pulled himself up to standing this way. His knees shook, as before, but he took one unsteady step to the side, and then another, so that he could pivot and then let himself fall back onto the bed. From there, he rapidly pushed himself back with his legs until he rested against the headboard, where he resumed watching her, grinning at her surprise.

Left at the foot of the bed, she shed her undergarments with almost vengeful speed and leapt up onto the bed on all fours, crawling toward him so rapidly that he laughed and shrank back, perhaps not entirely in jest. "A wild nymph," he murmured as she approached. His eyes were wide. She put her hands to his chest and ran them down its length again, feeling the thin hard muscle, the ridges of his ribs and hipbones. She kissed him hard, seizing the back of his head with a ferocity that startled even herself. She moved her lips down to his neck and kissed, then bit there. Again he moaned.

She pressed her hands against his shoulders, gently holding him steady against the headboard, then slowly slid her hand down his arms until, for the time, she could interlace her fingers with his. Silent, looking down at nothing in particular, she felt the play of the muscles in her hands against hers, the sudden jerks and contractions. His right arm jolted away; gently she bore down on that hand until it lay quivering against the coverlet again. She listened to their breathing.

"Does it disappoint you," she whispered suddenly, "that I'm so forward? If this isn't right..."

There had been something, a startled flicker of emotion, in his eyes, as he had watched her approaching.

She looked up again now. His lips were compressed, and his dark, angular eyebrows were drawn together with disquiet.

"I don't know," he said. "I don't know. It may be a lot to ask me... anything of what I'm thinking just now. None of this feels terribly real." A trace of his theatrical cadence returned at the end of the phrase, like a mechanism reestablishing itself.

"I feel the same," she said, still whispering, watching his face keenly. "But are you sure this is right?"

"Please don't ask me such a difficult question when we're already in... this position," he said, his face twisting.

"I'm sorry! I'm sorry. I just don't want to disappoint you."

"I can't imagine you could ever disappoint me," he said.

She thought this was too generous. Her breathing was shallow. "I don't know what to do."

"Don't say that. You're the only one here who has the least idea of how things should proceed at all."

She pushed out an uncomfortable laugh. In the silence that followed, he leaned forward shakily and sought her lips again, his head twisting through space until she had to give in and close the gap.

When she opened her eyes again, she found him meeting her gaze with disquieting intensity. She felt it like a little flame moving over her skin.

Silently she released his hands, and slowly moved hers down to his waistband. As he shivered under her touch, she undid his trousers, pushed them down his hips and off; his legs trembled tensely. Above, his arms were writhing wildly against the bed, through the air, and it roused her fear again: what if he was in a kind of panic... But no—when she looked up again, though his face showed the strain of trying to contain his body's movements, his eyes begged her to go onwards.

She smoothed one hand down one of his legs, heard his harsh exhalation of breath. Swiftly she swung one of her legs over his body—and then simply lay down along the full length of his body, front to front, pressing her cheek to his chest, hearing his heartbeat, wrapping her legs around his, stretching out her arms to grasp his wrists. Feeling below her all the warmth of his bare skin, his hardness. He moaned, and the sound hummed through her.

For long moments she lay like this, just wanting to feel him. She felt every motion of his wayward body, smelled the clean, warm scent of his skin; within her she nursed the ache to be touched more deeply.

Slowly, she sat up, straddling him, drawing his hands closer to her. He had sunk back against the pillows, and his eyes were glazed, heavy-lidded with desire. His body had grown lax, she realized dimly, the confusion of its movements slower, as if he were underwater. Once again she lifted his hands to her, and this time she traced all the contours of her body with them, her small breasts, the dimple of her navel, her full hips and rounded thighs, an anklebone, the arch of one foot. He gazed at her, lips parted, a tremor running through his frame every now and then.

Finally, she trailed his left hand around one hip and drew it towards the meeting of her thighs; with her thumb she extended two of his fingers and pushed them until she knew he could feel her wetness. She inhaled deeply, pleasure flooding up her body at his touch. His body jolted; his head fell to one side on the pillow. She did it again, and this time she released his other hand so that she could reach to stroke him, too. His moan shook her to her core.

The moments of touch that followed were torturously long, dream-like in their confusion; at every moment she felt as though one or the other of them would shatter. There was a kind of delicious strain in being required to control not only her own motions, but his—to orchestrate both their pleasure. Abstractedly she paused to watch once as his untethered right arm flailed on top of the coverlet, until he succeeded in thrusting it below one of the pillows under his head. Devilishly, she almost spoiled it by twisting her grasp upon him then, so that he cried out, very softly, and his arm thrashed under the pillow.

The pleasure mounted in her, and mounted: touching him, hearing him, watching his own pleasure transform that lean, elegant, ironic face.

Finally she could bear it no more: she sank down upon him and frantically rubbed her slickness all against his length, pushing closer and closer, stretching to kiss his lips, his jaw as she did so. Cautious even now, she did not take him into herself, but the contact, the heat, his hardness, his arrhythmic thrusts up against her, were all exquisite. Her awareness closed down, contracted into a kind of silent explosion, and then she was gasping over him as the waves of pleasure pushed through her again and again. Below her, she was dimly aware that he had reached his own crisis, jolting against her, sending heat across her belly, and the sound of his soft cry sent another stab of unbearable pleasure through her.

The room stilled. She lay upon him, tightly clasping his left hand, whose fingers stirred gently against her grasp even now.

She moved so that she could nestle her face more comfortably in the crook of his neck. The closeness of his skin, his face... Sleepily she pressed forward to kiss his cheek. He made a small sound, and she opened her eyes briefly to see him staring up at the ceiling, blinking. His body was so quiet now: still shifting often, yes, but the motions were slow, gentle; minor tremors rather than the sudden jolts and contortions of before. She relaxed against him, bathed in warmth, pleasure.

She became aware that he was tugging carefully at her hand. She opened her eyes again, loosening the fingers that had still held his, and watched from the corner of her eye as he haltingly lifted first his left, then his right hand—the right hand, which could not be controlled before—and brought them to rest in her hair.

"There," he breathed out, and the look of wonder in his eyes was so great that she had to close hers again. She pulled herself tighter against him.

They sank into darkness together. Her last perception was that, beyond the sound of his breath, she could hear a clock ticking softly somewhere in the room.

* * *

There was a sudden jolt. She woke slowly, blearily.

"Sorry," Michael was whispering. He sounded chagrined.

"What time is it?" she said after a moment. Her mouth was very dry and tasted foul.

"A quarter after four."

She took it in silently, reviewing. The jolt had been his body, she realized; he had convulsed under her, then collapsed back again.

"How long have you been awake?" she asked, mostly to have something to say.

"Maybe ten minutes." He sounded anxious, and she felt his left hand, which had still been resting against her hair, slide away and strike the bed.

"Mmm." She pushed herself up slowly, feeling thoroughly disreputable. Squinting down, she saw his apprehensive look and smiled tiredly, reaching down to cup his cheek. "Don't worry," she said, her voice cracking from dryness, "I'm like this when I wake up even under normal circumstances."

He managed a smile, and pressed his cheek into her hand.

"Please tell me," she murmured, rubbing her eyes with her other hand, "you have water somewhere here. And a cloth."

"Yes—there," he said, glancing to the side of the bed, and to her immense relief she saw on a nightstand, shadowed by the bedpost, a glass carafe full of water and several linen towels.

She drank first, and deeply; then she helped him sit up and sip carefully—a long straw had been left in the carafe for him. She moistened one of the towels and set about cleaning off each of them. She couldn't help lingering over his body a little when it came to his turn, but quickened her pace when she realized that both of them were flushing, and that little spasms were beginning to shake his torso. She kept her face studiously neutral.

Finally she threw the towel aside, and sat back on her heels. She ran her fingers across one of his collarbones as he looked at her, his arms splayed out to either side of him, twisting slowly. "You know I can't stay here," she said.

"Of course not," he said. His tone was even, but his face looked drawn.

"Will any of the servants be awake at this time?" she said carefully.

"I don't think so. Not in the main house."

"If anyone is... is there somewhere I could plausibly have fallen asleep without having been noticed? Somewhere nearer the party?"

"The music room," he offered. "If you leave the west door of the assembly room and keep following that hallway, it's at the end."

Who among the Byrnes was musical? she wondered deliriously. Perhaps Mrs. Byrne; she could imagine her drilling something out on a piano with military precision. "The music room," she repeated, considering. "I had too much champagne, and I fell asleep in the music room. I'm very embarrassed and now I simply must find my chamber—"

"In the gold hall," he put in eagerly; she realized that he was, again, trying to show that he was informed about goings-on.

"In the gold hall," she echoed. There was a pause as they could not avoid staring at each other. Her heartbeat was beginning to quicken, and there was a sick little feeling like panic in her stomach.

He broke the silence by saying, "You're going to have to help me dress again. Just my underclothes and my shirt and tie." The rest, he would have been able to take off by himself, she inferred.

Silently she climbed off the bed and went to put on her

slip, regather his clothes. He told her where there was a basket where she could hide the towel with other things to be washed. Again she could feel the weight of his gaze on her, and the rustling of his body and the ticking of the clock—it was on the dresser, she realized—seemed louder and louder.

When she was kneeling before him, buttoning his shirt methodically, as if pushing each button through its hole could tamp down her rising distress, and her distress at being distressed, he whispered, "What are we going to do?"

She didn't pause her motions. "I don't know, Mr. Byrne."

"*Please* call me Michael."

"I don't know, Michael," she repeated. There was a sour twist in her belly.

"I can't ask you to come back," he said.

"It certainly wouldn't be proper," she agreed hollowly.

"Would you *want* to come back," he persisted. He did not exactly say it as a question.

She finished his top button, straightened his collar, and began with his tie. Her lips were pressed tightly together. The soft slapping sound that his right arm made as it struck rhythmically against the pillows suddenly seemed enormously distracting, as if magnified. "You can leave the knot loose," he said stiffly.

"All right," she murmured, and did. Finally she looked at his face again: he was pale, and the lines around his eyes were deepened by tension. The image came to her suddenly of Winston Byrne, who, she thought, had much the same pattern of lines; but his would have come from squinting into the sun while riding.

She pressed her hands together. "I would," she whispered slowly, "like to come back, but I can't see how it would ever be possible." The enormous impossibility of the idea... it was like something she was much too tired to climb over.

But Michael's eyes had lit up. With a small shock she felt a slap on her wrist as he sought to grasp her with his better hand. After another try, he was able to grasp her hand and hold it, shaking.

"Miss De Vries," he began.

"You can call me Helena," she said, wearied by the absurdity as she said it.

"Helena," he said; she tried not to hear how caressingly he said it. "Helena, we have to try."

She could find nothing to say.

"You're only here for the summer. We can try... as long as you're willing to. And if you decide otherwise—well, you can simply stop coming. After all, you can go back East and forget you ever met me."

"That seems unlikely," she said. And she thought: *Do you really imagine I'm cold enough to do that?*

He gave a small laugh that sounded slightly hysterical.

"And how," she continued, "do you propose we would go about this?" She couldn't help how distant her tone had grown —the idea of leaving him alone again with his books and his little birds and his three rooms filled her with a quiet dismay... But then again, was it really any of her business?

The most dangerous thing, she thought, would be to hold herself responsible for his happiness.

"The art," he said with quiet urgency. "I can tell my mother about your work with your aunt. Mother can say that she heard about it at the party; she can say that she wants you to help us review the documentation of our holdings, arrange the redecoration of a gallery, curate a new collection, whatever... It's clear you like history, know it enough to like it, and my father may not know anything about it, but he likes things to *look* historical, if you hadn't noticed—"

"Your *mother?*" she interrupted incredulously. She thought of that proud, proud woman, with her fair hair pinned up smoothly on either side of her remote, oval face—like the formidable abbess of a medieval nunnery. For a woman like Mrs. Byrne to be complicit in arranging – what would you even call it?—arranging the *assignation* of her confined son... "Michael, I'm sorry, I haven't met your mother for more than a moment, but... surely it's a wild idea."

He paused. She stared down at his wavering hand, clasped around hers. "Mother is... complicated," he said, sounding as if he were agreeing with her. "But—and I hope this doesn't sound self-deluding—I know her to be partial to me in certain ways. I know it. And she takes a certain pride in knowing that... that I am happier than I might be otherwise. It was her who first gave me the finches to watch, you know. When I was very young."

"The finches?" she said, startled.

"Yes, the little birds in the conservatory. I know you noticed them."

She couldn't disagree. She ran her free hand through her short dark hair; her head was fairly reeling.

"She has these odd little outbursts of tenderness, you see... and she isn't nearly as old-fashioned as you might think."

"Michael, you can say that, but I think there's an ocean of difference between seeing to it that your son has finches to watch, and—and *this*." And she gestured to her near-nudity.

He looked uncomfortable; she knew she had scored a point. But he rallied. "Don't be silly—it doesn't have to be '*this*' that she knows about. I can just tell her that... you got bored of the party and went wandering to look at the art, the tapestries—" He interrupted himself, struck by a thought: "How *is* it that you've been swanning around unchaperoned tonight, anyway?"

Helena gave a short laugh. "My aunt begged off from the party to deal with a shipment of Turkish pottery being stone-walled by Customs. I came with a few other girls I'm supposed to be making friends with... A Mrs. Kincaid was supposed to be minding us, but she disappeared with a migraine after dinner."

"These fallen modern times." Michael shook his head. "Any-way, where were we. You were contemplating tapestries. You found me. We spoke for half an hour; we discovered interests in common; you charmed me. You suffered a headache from the champagne; you said good-bye and went away to sleep. And there, we've made a neat circle with the story about you falling asleep in the music room. You could even leave," he said with sudden, unseemly brightness, "a jewel or something behind in the music room... to prove you were there..." In his excitement, his torso was lurching from side to side, and his hand swung hers about. He added thoughtfully: "Besides, the De Vrieses are a family of excellent reputation."

"Of course you would know that," she said tensely. She didn't have to add, *And will that still be the case, if anyone else finds out about this, by the end of the summer?* She could it see it in the shadow that crossed his expression.

"You only feel... suspect," he went on, "because you know that '*this*' happened. To be brutally frank: *no one else would ever believe that it had.* To be even more frank, you might be... the only person I ever meet who would even conceive of it as a remote possibility."

Something, a sorrow, twisted inside of her. She bit her lips and looked aside.

The clock ticked on the dresser.

After a minute had passed, she said abruptly, recklessly, "We'll try it." She had worn herself out chasing down every path of possibility.

She thought of how, earlier in the night, all she had wanted was to see where the evening might go. And now, how it *had* gone...

Michael's eyes lit again, and he jerked at her hand excitedly. His other hand wavered through the air, brushing against her face twice before he managed to bring it to rest alongside her neck. "Helena," he said in a low voice.

"We have to do it properly," she said flatly. "Every step has to be irreproachable. You *must* be introduced to me as one of the Byrne sons. I'll be shy and remote. You—you can't *twinkle* at me the way you're twinkling right now," she said, crossly.

He laughed and swayed forward to kiss her. Reluctantly, she felt warmth spread through her at the renewed touch of his lips. But she pushed him away again, gently. "I'm being serious. Michael, listen. If we're to see each other, they'll want to chaperone us... at least for a while. It will be *hard* not to... not to show what you're feeling. And you might think highly of your mother's broad-mindedness, but I have my doubts. If she sees anything that she finds the least bit dubious... And you realize, it would very likely all reflect back on me, if anything were to be questioned?"

"Because I couldn't possibly wish anything for myself," he remarked bitterly.

"That's only one piece of it," she said, more gently. "Think... at the end of it, people would be more than happy to concede that an invalid man would... crave a young woman's attention. But what about the young woman's intentions? Especially when the invalid man is a son of one of the wealthiest families in America...?"

His face was twisted with dismay.

"People would say horrible things, Michael. Horrible. It would never be believed that I could feel anything like... natural affection for you."

He looked pale again. "You're right. Of course," he said, very low.

"I'm sorry. But we have to think about these things."

"Of course," he repeated. "But we *can* try." And his hand shook hers about a little, as if telling her to put her chin up.

"We can," she said, in a slightly warning tone. She didn't want to go on further. They would have days and days to think about everything that could possibly go wrong, and how very few chances there were for things to go right. And what was "right," anyway? Again she stopped herself thinking.

"Michael," she said, looking him in the eyes.

"Is it time to say good night?"

"I think it must be."

"Come closer, please."

She did, straddling him again, and he flung his arms around her, pulling her tightly to him in a spasmodic gesture. He pressed his nodding head against her chest, and she touched her fingers to the crown of his head, stroking him. He sighed deeply.

When he looked up again, she could not have named the expression on his face.

"Is there anything else you need before I go?" she asked quietly.

"No. Thank you." He released her, one arm simply dropping down heavily, the other springing up to shoulder height at his side, the hand gesticulating at the end of his wrist.

She dressed as quickly as she could manage. She bent to kiss him one last time before she unlocked the door again and stepped out. Behind her she could hear a soft storm of sound that must have been his body suddenly thrashing against the bed; it took all her resolve not to look back.

He hadn't asked her to promise she'd come back, and she hadn't promised anything.

As she hurried through the corridor just outside his room, she glanced warily at the one other door there. Surely it was a servant's room, so as to be within earshot of Michael's... but there was no sign of anyone having noticed anything.

She retraced her steps through the little conservatory, through the gallery full of books, back to the stairs. Then she remembered the damn bottle of champagne, left by the table hours ago. She doubled back to reclaim it; she could hide it somewhere closer to the party.

Returning to the stairs, she swore softly as she discovered the long-forgotten champagne glass; she reclaimed this, too.

The Tudor Hall was dark; someone had been by to turn out the lights. She wondered if Michael habitually kept late hours, so that the lights in his little wing beyond were often left on.

She looked down from the landing at the cavernous hall. It truly did look haunted now, the silhouettes of the heavy furniture severe and brooding, touched only with the bluish light of the night outside. She had a sudden sense of being a Shakespeare character, Hamlet perhaps, stalking about moodily, burdened with—here she almost snorted at herself—complex sorrows.

But truly, she wondered as she hurried through the hall, how many others could ever be said to have arrived in her position?

She wanted him to be happy. He was kind and witty and, in his strange way, elegant. He was so lonely. Notwithstanding his family's position, his circumstances were grotesquely unfair: to be treated like some kind of half-tolerated pet because of things about his body that he could not control... Picturing the way that his body writhed when he was taken by surprise or strong emotion, she had a sudden delirious notion that it was not because of physical affliction, but because of some spiritual transference of others' unkindness to him.

She wanted him to be happy, but she did not know if she could, or should, hold herself to be part of that happiness. What could they even hope for? She tried to picture strolling through a park with him, side by side as... It was unthinkable; she could not imagine it. War veterans might return home infirm, yes, and then vows to them must be honored—but to *choose* someone who was that way to begin with...

Her thoughts were running on so wildly. It had to be the lateness and strangeness of the night that was making them veer to the most drastic questions imaginable. She almost laughed when she thought about the engagement, her engagement, that had fallen apart over a year ago: she had been so awfully depressed about the whole thing, so unpredictable and uncharacteristically tremulous. In response, her parents had alternated periods of severity and disappointment with periods of anxious acquiescence, when they had said yes to just about everything that she had suggested might contribute to her recovery, to getting back on the track to a good marriage with a man of appropriate status.

And see how she had repaid her parents' hopes tonight.

Well, no one could say he wasn't *wealthy*... Here she restrained herself from laughing again.

At least the idea of a friendship might be entertained. There, finally, was a reasonable conclusion. But even then, her mouth twisted bitterly as it struck her that they would never even be able to exchange correspondence frankly: he would need someone else to write and post his letters for him. Even a telephone he would need help with, and someone might always be in the room, listening...

And yet, and yet: how could she ignore him, having met him, however briefly? Having known that she could feel so passionately about him—having known that not only friendship, but desire could flow so naturally between them. No, she could never believe there was something unnatural about what had happened between them. It was only, only, what *anybody* else at all would think...

She realized that she had found her way to the music room; she fumbled for the light. Green velvet settee, gleaming grand piano. Her head was spinning, and she felt chilly and almost sick with fatigue. She put a hand to her mouth and cursed herself for not saying good-bye to him more sweetly.

Why was she here? Yes, his silly, novelistic remark about leaving something behind, to show she had been here. She would have to remember to make a point of asking after it when she woke again in a few hours. She fumbled at the bodice of her black dress, where large, faceted crystal beads lined the neckline. One came loose easily, and she weighed it for a moment in her hand before tossing it lightly—"For Michael," she said softly—to land on the settee. It glinted conspicuously.

She put out a hand to turn off the lights again, then turned back briefly; the crystal was invisible now. Somehow she had hoped to see it still.

Never mind; she shook herself and hastened back to find her room, where she would lie awake until the grey light of false dawn, thinking of the resonance of Michael's lilting voice, the uncertain grip of his hands, the light in his dark, sharp, sad eyes; wondering if he, too, lay awake in a room that after all was so close by that she could have run to him in a few minutes; wondering when they would see each other next, and how she could keep from running to him when they did.

Part II: Hortus Conclusus

Hortus conclusus: An enclosed, inviolate garden ... in reference to the Song of Solomon.

— *The Oxford English Dictionary*

Hortus conclusus soror mea, sponsa, hortus conclusus, fons signatus.

A garden enclosed is my sister, my spouse; a garden enclosed, a fountain sealed up.

— Song of Solomon, *The Vulgate Latin Bible*

Helena knew the moment he arrived. Though his arrival was always arranged with the utmost of discretion, still she knew. She had her back to the audience, was digging about in a box of excelsior to extract the next artifact that would accompany Aunt Delia's lecture on Ottoman ceramics. Her fingertips touched the cool rim of the dish through the nest of shredded wood fiber, and she froze.

She thought to herself: *No one else will have heard it*—the slight creak that she knew came from the right-hand post of his chair, where the back met the seat. Someone might have heard it, but no one else would have marked it, certainly not amid the soft sea of throat-clearings, seat-shiftings, and program-rustlings that arose from the crowd of some of California's wealthiest citizens, gathered on the grounds of the Byrne mansion.

But she had heard the creak, and she marked it, and she knew that he had arrived. She could not control the shivering run of pleasure and anxiety that went through her.

Aunt Delia, with her rich, plummy voice, was instructing the audience to note the influence of blue-and-white Chinese porcelain on the next piece they were to see. She paused significantly, and Helena could see from the corner of her eye that Delia was giving her a smile.

She swallowed, pressed her fingers carefully about the dish, withdrew it from its box, and turned with conscious grace to hold the broad Turkish dish up for the audience to see, with its bold, intricate patterns of fan-shaped flowers and arabesques.

The late afternoon sunlight set the glazes to glowing with benevolent warmth: cobalt blue, white, and coral red. A wave of appreciative exclamations and murmurs went through the crowd, and Helena smiled slightly, as if accepting tribute on behalf of the dish. She kept her eyes lowered.

This was a contemporary example, Aunt Delia was explaining, and yet its heritage was clear. They might see its forebears —infinitely more precious, spanning centuries—if they were to attend the opening of her museum next year. For now, this fine inheritor of tradition would well serve today's discussion.

Only when Helena felt the weight of the audience's attention on her dissipating, drawn back to the magnetic figure of her aunt, did she lift her eyes. With careful composure, she swept her gaze across the ranks of seated men and women in their suits and gowns, sheltered from the sun by the long pavilion draped with white muslin, until finally she looked beyond the last row to see Michael Byrne sitting there in the shade. Behind him stood Karl, his man, one hand still resting lightly on the push-bar at the back of Michael's wheelchair.

She controlled her expression, but her heart beat faster. She forced herself to breathe out slowly. Michael was smiling at her, his head tilting slightly toward one shoulder; she imagined that even from here, she could see his dark eyes glinting. The easeful fondness of his smile made her face warm.

She looked back toward Aunt Delia, and seeing a slight nod, began to walk slowly toward the audience, proffering the dish for their examination. Aunt Delia began to describe with great liveliness the apprenticeship of an Ottoman potter of the

16th century. As she conjured the bustling streets of the walled lake town where the apprentice shaped vessels and concocted glazes, Helena walked up and down the rows, pausing when asked to allow Mrs. or Mr. Whoever to examine more closely the banquet dish she carried. She smiled and answered their whispered questions, none of them very difficult.

Moving about the crowd, casting her gaze about to see if anyone else wanted to have a look at the dish, she had the perfect pretext now to keep stealing glances at Michael. Often she caught him gazing back at her again, but other times, he was watching Aunt Delia with pleasure.

Every time they met again, it was if she had to sketch him back into reality, to confirm for herself that he really existed— particularly on the exceedingly rare, and therefore somewhat surreal, occasions when he appeared in public. He was lean and dark, the man resting in the wheelchair of wicker and wood, with a face that she knew was weathered by tension rather than by exposure to the elements. He wore a well-cut camel suit and a panama hat. She saw, with a twist of complex emotion, that today he was strapped into his wheelchair: one broad band of brown leather across his chest, one more at each of his wrists, securing his arms to the armrests. Nonetheless, he was listing to one side, and she could see that his arms jerked and tugged at the straps on his wrists, twisting the fabric of his suit.

She forced herself to keep moving. "The treasured blue glazes of Chinese pottery," Aunt Delia was saying, her voice hypnotic, enticing, "were actually *Persian* in origin, a gemlike gift of the Silk Road... translated into an Oriental vernacular, and then imitated again, in turn, by the artisans of the Ottomans..." This revelation merited several more prolonged examinations of the dish that Helena carried. While she paused to let heads bend over the dish, she stole more glances away. She took in the curl of dark hair just visible below the brim of his hat, the quick movements of his eyes and occasional twist of his mouth as his body shifted restlessly against its restraints.

But she turned away before she reached the last row. With ceremonious grace, she proceeded back toward Aunt Delia, who stood resplendent before a trellis of bougainvillea. Aunt Delia was concluding: she hoped that they would all enjoy the hospitality of the Byrnes for the duration of this fine afternoon, that she might have the pleasure of answering their questions over champagne, and that she hoped to welcome them to further explore the wonders of the Silk Road when her museum held its gala in the fall of next year.

Amid applause and a lifting breeze, Delia inclined her head graciously to her listeners. Helena stood to one side, watching. As soon as the applause had faded and the crowd began migrating toward the courtyard where canapés and champagne awaited, she turned to replace the Turkish dish. The light was starting to turn a darker shade of gold, and the breeze bore the freshness of the approaching Californian evening.

"That went very well, don't you think?" Aunt Delia said. Helena paused in repacking the dish to smile up at her.

Delia was a magnificent woman, almost six feet tall, broad-shouldered, with thick curling chestnut-colored hair and heavy features. Her eyes were large, sleepy, and continually amused. She liked to dress the part of a priestess of art, and today wore a loosely draped Poiret gown, blood-red, with a woven pattern of circular Grecian keys, black, running across the breast, and a fanciful fringe at the hem.

Helena, by contrast, wore a simple dove-grey gown, notable mainly for its fluidity of form. "You charmed them to bits," she said. "They were like serpents winding around your wrists by the end. If you had had milk to pour in the dish, they would have been lapping it up."

Aunt Delia laughed. "Now, now."

"Really!" Helena protested. "That was just right. Not too dry, not too light. *Just* enough to challenge their sensibilities— you know, make them feel smart and maybe a bit dangerous in their tastes—and get them wanting more."

"Speaking of—" Aunt Delia said in a lower tone.

Helena turned to see Michael approaching, Karl pushing his chair, and blushed.

"Mr. Byrne," Aunt Delia called in greeting.

He was smiling that smile again. "Miss De Vries; Miss Helena," he returned, inclining his head, and then addressed Aunt Delia: "How is it that you haven't been swept off yet by a crowd of admirers?"

"Did Helena put you up to this?"

"Oh, please, you know your talk was excellent. Thank you for it, really. It's rare to get such a vivid sense of both the particulars of individual lives, and, you know, something like the scope of centuries. All those cultures and aspirations mingling and seizing and surging forward with one another... And all of it coming to rest in something that we might otherwise just call a pretty dish with flowers. Oh! And it was well-done to bring it around to cobalt—there's something mesmerizing about pursuing a line of thought through a single material. An alchemical viewpoint, maybe."

"Mr. Byrne," Aunt Delia said with warmth, "thank you. It means a great deal to hear so much from such a student of history as yourself. But look—I'm very sorry, but they *have* finally realized that I'm shirking the canapés. My dears, you must excuse me. Helena, you ought to show Mr. Byrne..." And she hurried away toward the courtyard, raising her arms in a placatory gesture toward the small cluster of people who beckoned her onwards urgently.

"It's good to see you again, Miss De Vries," Michael said to Helena. His smile creased his eyes deeply.

Helena had taken a moment to collect herself, and so was ready to greet him. "Mr. Byrne. And hello, Karl." The trim, bald man with the blonde moustache gave her a brief smile and a murmured greeting. She addressed Michael again. "Did you want to see...?" And she gestured toward the Turkish dish.

"Yes, please." And Karl wheeled him forward until he could bend over the trestle table where it rested in its box.

Helena watched him: the slight parting of his lips, the curve of his neck as he leaned forward against the strap over his chest, the constant opening and closing of his fingers, involuntary yet somehow expressive. She found herself thinking, *If his wrists were not tied down today, I could take his hand and help him feel the dish...* Dimly, she was aware that Karl had stepped back a little distance, as if they required privacy. Not for the first time that summer, she wondered how much he knew.

"It is remarkable," Michael was saying, "how alike they are..." It wasn't entirely clear what he was referring to.

He looked up and found her watching him. He returned her gaze and then, after a moment, said softly, "You never like it when I have these on, do you?" And he indicated the straps around him with his chin.

Startled, she said, "How did you know what I was thinking?"

"Oh, you get this look. Distantly disapproving."

She gave a small, embarrassed laugh, and looked aside. "Well... they don't look very comfortable."

His head had dropped forward onto his chest. When he was able to lift it again, he said, "They're comfortable enough. Sometimes it even feels better than, you know, just flopping about all the time. The whole point is to make me look a bit less mad."

"But they make you look *more* mad," Helena pointed out. "You look as if you're about to be carted off to an institution for the criminally insane."

He laughed. "Sometimes it flatters a man's ego to be thought of as dangerous, Miss De Vries. I have vanishingly few chances to do so."

She made a face at him. "But really," she said, more softly, "I suppose I don't like it... because I don't like the idea that you can't get in and out of your chair yourself." She knew he could, under the right circumstances. "It *is* like you're a prisoner."

"Well," he said reasonably, "that's what Karl helps me for."

"I know, but—" She made an exasperated noise and gave up.

She had first met Michael Byrne by chance three months earlier that summer: the unknown Byrne, the unknown son of one of the country's wealthiest families, who was more or less confined to a back wing of their estate in southern California because he had been afflicted since birth with palsy. He was clever and kind and inquisitive; he surprised her with how much he could make her could laugh. And memories of his resonant voice, of his warm, mobile mouth, of touches from his trembling hands, made her thoughts melt and loosen whenever they came over her.

But the facts, the uncongenial facts, could not be changed. He could not walk unaided; he could not dress nor feed himself; and most of his family treated him as if he were an inconvenient ghost, whose occasional appearances at gatherings were to be tolerated for as brief a period as possible, and never remarked upon.

And yet, again and again since their first meeting, Helena had found herself confounded in trying to express her care, her concern for Michael without retreading "difficulties" that he had long since ceased to think of as difficulties, if indeed he had ever done so. There were so many occasions when she misunderstood, or unthinkingly imposed her own sense of how his dignity or comfort ought to be managed. It made her feel awkward, even arrogant. And yet she still could not shake the underlying sense that his life ought to be better than it was.

She lifted her gaze to find him watching her with that look

that suggested that he knew where her thoughts were running. But what he said was, "You're leaving soon, aren't you, Helena?"

Her face went cold. She thought at once, *Why must he make things so difficult?* But then she felt the injustice of that thought.

"Yes," she said hesitantly. "They're expecting me back in Philadelphia in a few weeks."

"Two weeks and six days," he said: not an admonition, simply an observation. His head was wavering from side to side, but he kept his eyes on her.

"Yes," she said.

"Well," he said, "I have enjoyed our friendship. I hope you'll come to see me at least once more before you leave." His hands twisted slowly against their straps.

"Well," she said, a little too eagerly, "you know I might come back again. In January, maybe February. Since things are going so well with, with Aunt Delia's museum. And Philadelphia is so dreadful in February."

"So you've said," he replied.

She darted a glance at Karl, who was looking off soberly at the terraced gardens above them, hands clasped behind his back. She wished she could shoo him off to the kitchens to refresh himself; she wished she could take Michael by the shoulders and beg him to tell her what he meant by all of this, by the steady affection in his eyes, by his bewilderingly un-expectant composure. It gave her nothing to grasp onto; it put all the weight onto her, she thought. She resisted the urge to twist at the folds of her gown.

She lifted her head at a noise: a pair of groundsmen were

approaching with a cart to carry away Aunt Delia's demonstration pieces. Not caring how inelegant it might be, she hastily indicated the servants and said to Michael, "Would you like to see the dish one more time before I have to tuck it away?"

"That's all right, thank you. I think Karl and I will take a turn around the grounds, now," he said. Of course there was no question of him attending the party. His body was moving more rapidly now, his head dipping from side to side, making it difficult for him to keep his gaze on her, and his knees were drawing upwards in his seat. She didn't know if this was belying the composure of his voice, or if he had simply been startled by the arrival of the servants.

"Michael," she began, and moved towards him until she could grasp one of his hands with both of hers; she couldn't think clearly enough to guess whether this would be hidden from both Karl and the approaching groundsmen. But she held onto him, feeling the irregular pressure of his spasming fingers, and she watched as he lifted his eyes to hers, until his head fell towards his chest again. And then she released him and stepped away to busy herself with repacking the dish, only half-listening as the servants greeted Michael cheerily—for they were all fond of him, the servants.

As she moved away disconsolately toward the babble of voices in the courtyard, she held onto that last look in his eyes: dark, perversely opaque with the light of the setting sun, as if the idealized golden gleam were a barrier between her and any interpretation of what he wanted, what he expected, what he hoped for.

* * *

At the party, she thought, *Sorry, Aunt Delia*, and, rather than making herself available to any of the number of guests who might have liked to hold forth at her about their interest in her aunt's work, retired as soon as possible to the company of Lily Tedford-Blank. Lily was a short, plump, white-blonde girl with an odd manner of perpetual distraction. She was very pretty, but most people seemed to find her long silences off-putting. They suited Helena admirably in her present mood. As the evening grew bluer and lamps were lit, she sheltered alongside Lily at the edge of the busy courtyard, lugubriously sipping from a glass of champagne.

For the first time, it occurred to her that many people might now see Helena herself in a similar light to Lily: vague, elusive, apparently uninterested in men. She thought to make a joke of it to Lily, but when she turned to look at Lily's profile, with her upturned nose and rosebud lips, she found she had nothing fit to say.

Here's the trouble, she imagined herself saying to Lily, in-stead. *In this very peculiar situation, I feel as if I'm playing the part of the man.*

The moon is made of silver glass tonight, Lily might say, or somesuch.

Precisely, Helena would say. *You see, conceited it may be, but—I feel as if I have seduced an innocent, and now it is my respon-sibility to decide what to make of it, and that is exactly the sort of scenario in whose management a nice young woman is devastatingly uninstructed.*

Swans mate for life, Lily might suggest.

Why can't he just say what he really *wants me to do?* Helena would say, before she could stop herself complaining.

Of course he can't do that, Lily would say; and there Helena's reverie ended, unhelpfully as it had begun.

"You're a good sort, Lily," Helena said finally, and out loud. Lily turned to her with a look of mild surprise, which then transformed into a look of obscurely knowing humor. "Do you find most things funny, Lily?" Helena found herself saying.

After a moment, Lily smiled with surprising warmth. "I do."

Helena smiled back at her, and touched the other girl's wrist briefly. "Good night, Lily."

"Good night." And Helena moved off into the crowd.

* * *

By the time that Mrs. Byrne found her later, Helena was slightly drunk and pretending to listen to golfing talk among people whose names she couldn't remember. But she felt a touch on her shoulder, and turned aside to find Catherine Byrne, Michael's mother, looking at her levelly.

Helena straightened, and Mrs. Byrne said, "Won't you come with me for a moment, Miss De Vries?" She nodded mutely and followed after.

"It has been a great pleasure to make a deeper acquaintance of your aunt," Mrs. Byrne said, once they had reached a quieter spot. She was small and firmly built, with a remote, oval face and blonde hair parted down the middle; she made Helena think of some of the more severe paintings of medieval saints. "I have you, and... Michael, to thank for expanding our circle in this way. It's been my aspiration for some time for our family to take a greater interest in the arts."

Helena marshalled a smile, trying to hide how unsettling she found both the name "Michael" on Mrs. Byrne's lips, and the hesitation that accompanied it. *She doesn't like to acknowledge him, even to somebody who already knows him.*

She forged on: "The pleasure is ours, I can assure you, Mrs. Byrne. You've been most generous. We couldn't have asked for a more perfect setting for Aunt Delia's lecture today. A true garden of Babylon."

"I'm glad to hear you think so," Mrs. Byrne replied. "Building up the grounds from a pebble-strewn slope has been quite the undertaking, as you can imagine. So I'm contented we could provide you with agreeable circumstances under which to enjoy a fine California evening... do I understand correctly that you are departing our coast soon?"

"Yes," said Helena carefully, "in about three weeks."

"You must be terribly busy, between planning your departure, and your admirable efforts to assist your aunt." Mrs. Byrne's pale eyes were unnervingly cool and steady, and she made little effort to appear moved by the pleasantries they exchanged.

"Oh, it's no great trouble. We've both known the end of my summer idyll was coming, of course, and we'd planned for it accordingly—though it is always a temptation to say yes to just one more project for Aunt Delia." *What was she about?* Helena wondered.

"Well," said Mrs. Byrne, "only if it won't be an imposition, I wonder if you might like to do me the favor of taking tea with me sometime next week."

"Oh," said Helena, who made a habit of spending as little time in close quarters with Mrs. Byrne as was practicable. "Why, yes, I think I could..." she said slowly. She wished she hadn't drunk quite so much.

"Tuesday, perhaps?" Mrs. Byrne suggested, pressing her opening.

"Tuesday would be fine," Helena said obediently. In fact she had wanted to attend a meeting with Aunt Delia and the museum's architect, and oversee the inventory of a new shipment of pieces, but she didn't see how she could say no.

"We could even send a driver for you, if you think that yours might be occupied," Mrs. Byrne offered, though not with unseemly eagerness.

"Well, I don't know that that would be necessary, but it's very kind... I can let you know?"

"Yes, do; you can call. It *would* be pleasant to see you under quieter circumstances. But of course, if something more urgent arises, there's no trouble. Think about it, and don't let me take any more of your time now. Do enjoy the evening, Miss De Vries." For the first time, Mrs. Byrne gave a small smile that actually touched her eyes.

"Thank you—" And Helena watched, bemused, as Mrs.

Byrne withdrew, her small figure cleaving smoothly through the crowd.

* * *

An hour or so later, in the car on the way back to Aunt Delia's home, Helena clasped her hands about Delia's arm and rested her head upon her shoulder. Aunt Delia looked down at her inquiringly and touched her hair. Helena opened her mouth to say something, but at once the idea of shouting to be heard above the noise of the drive seemed exhausting. She merely held Delia's arm tighter, feeling her comforting warmth. She would not, she thought, think of Michael's eyes in the sunset; and thereby, of course, thought of him again. She closed her eyes, letting the wind push into her face and batter her head empty again.

* * *

She and Michael had been able to see each other that summer more often than she had ever expected to, and therein lay the trouble. If they had only had the one night in May, maybe they would each have been able to hold it off as a delirious dream, impossible to replicate. *I have had a most rare vision*, as Bottom had it; *I have had a dream—past the wit of man to say what dream it was.*

But the universe had supported their friendship: once a formal introduction between Michael and Helena had been managed, Mrs. Byrne had held tight to the resultant thread of connection with Delia De Vries, who, though eccentric, bore a nimbus of cultural authority and sophistication that the Byrnes as a whole struggled to cultivate. The Byrne *paterfamilias*, a former prospector, was notoriously hard-edged and tight-fisted. Mrs. Byrne's task was to smooth him out, at least in the eyes of the public, and she pursued it with the deliberation of a panther setting each velvet foot one after the other. The brassy, irascible Mr. Byrne would never, say, make Congress—but the admiration of more Congressmen could never go astray. Nor could a reputation of investing in institutions of public benefit: schools, clinics, museums.

All of this meant that throughout the summer, Delia and Helena had had invitations to dine with the Byrnes or appear at their parties several times a month to start; and later, once Mrs. Byrne had conceived of hosting a lecture series for Delia in the Byrne gardens, even more often.

Not every visit allowed Helena to see Michael, for she was afraid to ask after him too much. But more often than not, Mrs. Byrne herself suggested that Helena might call on him, although the indirectness with which she did it soured Helena's stomach. It was as if Mrs. Byrne took care to avoid speaking of him too seriously or forthrightly. It was as if they were *all*, Helena realized once with dismay, tiptoeing around his presence in the midst of the household.

Except for Aunt Delia, of course: after making his acquaintance, she spoke of him openly and glowingly, even when Helena could tell that Mrs. Byrne's face had frozen into a brittle expression in reaction. What was it that she saw in Mrs. Byrne's eyes, then? Could it be fear?

Once, Mrs. Byrne was speaking of her eldest son, Patrick, who lived with his family in Colorado and oversaw a significant portion of the family corporation's interests in mining and timber. She was describing a difficult decision that he was weighing about how far to go in diversifying their interests in minerals, when Delia put in, "You know, I wonder what Michael would have to say about it. It has struck me that he's really quite insightful about your family business, as he is in other things."

The look that emerged on Mrs. Byrne's face in response to this was so strained, even appalled, that even Delia realized that she had overstepped, and hurried to make the kind of apology and diverting remarks that she usually avoided.

In these interactions, Helena felt as if she had been pressed into a paper version of herself and set into a frame: devoid of color or conviction, unable to take a step in one direction or another. She felt as if the least remark might betray her true feelings, that her guilt would blaze up Biblically behind her words. In these moments, even her memories of Michael seemed fragmented, confused, diminished: what could have happened between them to make her feel so? Had it really happened to begin with?

And so the best times, the times of almost painful brightness, were those when finally, finally, Helena was able to see Michael again, to come to find him in the sunny, book-lined gallery where he spent most of his time, with newspapers and books untidily spread out on the table before him and Karl playing solitaire or napping discreetly in a corner. She would come up the small, dear flight of stairs where she had first found Michael, and step down the hallway to see him wrenching his head up to watch her approach. He would be leaning forward in his wheelchair, his arms beginning the frantic waving dance that accompanied moments of excitement for him.

When she saw his wide smile of greeting, when she first heard his voice again: these were the things that brought color flooding back, that made the world settle into place around her. How hard it was to not go rushing to him, then, to be circumspect in her friendly graciousness. When she drew close enough to him, she felt as if she were frantically sending off signals with her eyes: *I've missed you, how I've missed you, I would kiss you a hundred times now, if I could.*

Her signals were received—she thought—and reflected back in aura of peaceable contentment that radiated out from Michael as if from a sleeping cat. "Good afternoon, Miss De Vries," he'd say; and the resonance of his voice set off a chord in her heart. And he would invite her to discuss the day's news with him, or a concert she'd seen with Aunt Delia that weekend, or the Antarctic travails of the Norseman Amundsen. Michael kept a framed photograph of the explorer's grave, shamanic visage, wreathed in furs. Helena shared Michael's fascination with such explorers, who persisted to unimaginably remote reaches of the Earth; but she wondered, too, how much more depth of longing such expeditions held for Michael, who had rarely traveled even a few miles from his family home. "If

I were ever to go to Europe, I would love to see it with my own eyes," he might say of a painting or a medieval fortress, but the tone of his voice was light, abstract: he knew it would never happen.

Helena herself had never yet been to Europe. But when she turned the pages in books of paintings for Michael, or passed on to him postcards of artifacts that Aunt Delia had given her, and heard his exclamations of delight and curiosity, she had to imagine it: her first voyage to Europe, *their* first voyage to Europe, her and Michael traveling together -train, steamer, train again. London, Paris, Prague, Vienna. Stoic, dependable Karl would see to Michael's comfort, while she and Michael devised their itinerary. It would be a gift that they could give each other, for they would each be seeing it for the first time, together. Michael might need to be carried sometimes, but she was sure it could be done—surely there were arthritic grandes dames and gouty American bourgeois who required such services on their trips about the Continent. And then she had to chide herself for such a comparison. Michael was limited in his abilities, yes, but he was not fragile nor frail; his health was vigorous, and she knew that when he was alone with Karl, he made as much effort as he could to walk and move about by himself as he could.

And her thoughts would tumble onward, imagining *café au lait* breakfasts together, her pushing Michael's chair under misty boulevards of pollarded plane trees, or down Mediterranean country lanes with cypresses standing sentry against luminous skies of dusk-blue... And so on, until she ran up against the impossibility of it all, the infuriating, stupid impossibility.

She would only realize that she had grown quiet, her eyes absently fixed on the familiar sight of Michael's left hand clasped about the wrist of his more wayward, wavering right arm, when Michael would push himself up in his chair with his legs and say with amusement, "Miss De Vries, whatever are you thinking about?"

She couldn't say anything, then; there was far too much to say. So she would shake her head and smile, and invite him to continue. His dark eyes would watch her keenly; but he would not ask further after her thoughts.

When it came down to it, it was not about Europe, and it was never about what Michael could or could not do. It was about what *she* could not do. Once, she was watching him in the mellowing afternoon light, watching the strange dance of his body as spasms cast his limbs about, while he chatted on quietly, unperturbed. In that moment, she longed to take hold of his hands and say, "Do you know how much *time* we are wasting? How much time we are being *made* to waste?" So much time when she could not say what she really wanted to say, so much time when they could not touch each other. While Michael seemed, merely and deeply, to be content in her presence, she felt as if she were burning up alongside him.

Karl was no tell-tale, she could guess, but to be indiscreet before him was still unthinkable. The idea instantly brought the image of her mother's lips to her mind, precisely forming the words, "Your reputation."

And so it was both a burden and a relief on the occasions when she arrived in Michael's gallery to find that—"Hi, Miss De Vries!"—his younger brother, Lewis, was also there visiting. Lewis had just finished college and taken up a position as a partner in the Byrnes' Los Angeles office; he shared an apartment there with a college chum, but drove out to the Byrne mansion with a frequency that, Helena thought, reflected well on him.

The four Byrne brothers shared their father's distinctive nose, but where the three eldest—Patrick, Michael, and his identical twin, Winston—were lean, rangy, and dark, Lewis bore their mother's oval face and fair coloring. Helena could admit that Lewis, like Michael, was funny and easily endearing, but she found it hard not to think of him as a little brother, though he was one year older than her. Unlike Michael, he was distractible—dreamy, a little flighty. She found herself growing impatient sometimes with his sociable ramblings and half-finished thoughts.

Once, for example, Helena had been speaking with Michael of the architect's growing plans for Aunt Delia's museum. "And so," she was saying, "there'll be a series of little peristyles, or cloisters, open to the air, as if you were walking through a succession of Roman homes—"

Lewis put in then, "And the architect? What's his name?"

"The architect," Helena said, a little touchily, "is a woman, and her name is Jane Montague." She saw Michael smiling to himself.

"Oh!" said Lewis. "So your aunt will be saving herself a

bundle on architect's fees, I imagine." He said it with an air of such innocent discovery—as if Aunt Delia had merely made an unconventional but commendably frugal business decision—that it was almost difficult to be irritated with him.

And yet, Lewis's fondness for Michael was so evident, frank, and refreshing that it filled the space with a kind of playful ease, as if a kitten had been invited into their midst. He would draw up a chair alongside Michael and loll half on his brother's shoulder, one arm slung around his back, not caring how often one of Michael's sudden uncontrolled movements dislodged him. He teased Michael lightly if he saw that Michael had accidentally damaged another of his books: "Oh, when are they going to take away your library card? And anyway, don't you think you've already read enough books for one lifetime?"

Once, Helena arrived in the gallery to find it empty, for, she realized as she heard voices floating in from one of the open windows, Lewis had taken Michael down to the gardens outside. She hastened to the window and leaned out over the false balcony that extended only a few inches beyond. On the broad-flagged terrace beneath, bordered by acacia trees and pink-flowering oleander, she saw Lewis racing back and forth, pushing the bulky wooden wheelchair before him, while Michael laughed helplessly, doubled so far over his knees that his arms were trapped awkwardly in his lap. Lewis completed a dramatic hairpin turn, sending Michael lurching to one side, and then came about to a stop, collapsing alongside the wheelchair on one of the flagstones, his chest heaving with breath and his arms outflung. It thrilled her to hear Michael's uncontrolled laughter carry on, echoing off the flagstones.

After half a minute, Lewis collected himself, coming up to his knees and turning to help his brother sit up straight again. She was deeply touched when she saw that Lewis even put out a thumb to carefully wipe tears of laughter away from under Michael's eyes. The younger brother then sat back, rested his arms upon his drawn-up knees, and proceeded to speak to Michael in an attitude of confidence for quite some time. Michael's head was bent towards him and lolled from side to side on occasion, so Helena could see his face only in glimpses, but he seemed to be listening gravely and fondly, before beginning to respond.

They talked like this for a while before Lewis rose up and flung his arms around his brother, in, Helena thought, a sudden outburst of gratitude or affection. She wished she could hear their voices more clearly, but she could only hear the rising and falling strains of Lewis's tenor and Michael's baritone. There followed another exchange, more playful this time: Lewis seemed to be pleading with Michael over something, or egging him on, for Michael shook his head laboriously a few times, laughing again, before finally seeming to agree.

Lewis came around to the front of Michael's wheelchair and held out both hands. Helena could see from how he adjusted his stance that he was bracing himself, but it still surprised her when he reached out, firmly grasped the undersides of Michael's forearms, and helped his brother to step out of his wheelchair.

Michael rose, shaking, his back and knees deeply bent, and his head bobbing rapidly. She could see the tension running through his whole frame, and he could not keep his right hand grasped around Lewis's arm; the hand twisted and curled to one side, fingers twitching, which seemed to distract him for a moment. But Lewis kept hold of him, standing square and steady, and so Michael was able to proceed forward, hesitantly at first, his steps coming in small, fumbling jerks, but with more confidence as they moved on. As they neared one end of the courtyard, he was able to stand straighter, his legs pushing him upward with more strength; she could see a broad smile on Lewis's face.

They were beginning to manage the turn around when a maid cleared her throat behind Helena. She started, then composed herself. The maid smiled and reported that Miss Delia had asked after her. Helena gave her thanks and turned away from the window to follow the maid back to the main hall, trying to dismiss the sense that she had been caught spying.

After this incident, she resolved to be more patient with Lewis. She had to admit that he seemed to be fond of her, too, quickly coming to include her in his light-hearted teasing, and asking her about her friends and family back in Philadelphia, or her brief time living in New York. And so finally it became a relief when she caught him during one social function or another, for once she had, she knew that she would be provided with undemanding conversation and an excuse for not making herself available to other men.

The one thing about Lewis of which she could not make

heads or tails was his college friend and apartment-mate. John Daniel Plainsborough was tall and chestnut-haired, and frequently at Lewis's elbow at parties. None of his features individually were remarkable, but Helena thought that some combination of his demeanor and coloring conferred on him a dark glow of attractiveness. He kept his hands folded behind his back at most times. Altogether, he had a faint air of superiority, or even menace, and yet he approached Helena with the most bewildering series of behaviors, a seeming parody of seduction: frequent winks to begin with, and then, when she seemed adequately disconcerted, long knowing looks about nothing that she could identify. When this phase, too, seemed to have had its desired effect on her—whatever that was supposed to be—he proceeded to ignore her as often as possible. This suited her better than everything that had come before.

Interestingly, she could not tell if John Daniel had ever met Michael. When Lewis mentioned Michael's name in conversation among the three of them, John Daniel did not seem to react at all. But then, perhaps it was *her* of whom John Daniel was uncertain: perhaps he *had* met Michael, but was uncertain of the extent to which he ought to be keeping mum about him in Helena's presence.

Altogether, it was a bundle of little mysteries... but not one in which she took any deep interest. Her thoughts, after all, if they were not with Aunt Delia and the work of her museum, remained with Michael.

* * *

On a very few occasions, she thought that she had caught Michael watching her with a line of frustration between his brows, a tension about the set of his mouth; but once she had looked at him more closely, it was gone. And if it had been there to begin with, perhaps he had been reacting only to the rigors of his body.

* * *

Two days after Aunt Delia's lecture in the Byrne gardens, Helena accompanied her to the site where the museum was to be erected, on a hillside about an hour's drive from Los Angeles. The outlines of the foundations had been freshly excavated, exposing the tawny bedrock of sandstone and shale. Materials lay about in great canvas-swathed heaps: steel piles to be driven, gravel, sacks of sand. Humble stuff; the glimmering slabs of white Carrara marble would not begin arriving till much later in the year, when Helena had gone.

As it was eleven o'clock, workmen were taking their rest in the shade of oaks, eating out of lunch-pails and squinting up at the two women standing at the rim of the site. Delia wore a broad hat of fine pale straw and a tabard-cut silk dress of a terracotta color, its breast heavily embellished with brass beads and turquoises. Helena wore a cloche and a crisp cotton dress with a natty print of grey, white, and blue.

Helena thought that the raw footprint of the foundations, glowing under the strong white-gold sun, resembled nothing so much as an archaeological excavation. She spent some pleasant minutes picturing history as a looped configuration, each generation digging up remnants of the past and reconstituting them according to modern imagination. She imagined, with a pleasant sense of melancholy, a wind blowing golden dust through the toppled pillars of her aunt's museum, some centuries hence. Perhaps young lovers, calling to each other in some incomprehensible linguistic descendant of English, Greek, or Chinese, would go scrambling through the ruins to find a shady spot to enjoy their lunch...

But when she looked up at Aunt Delia, she found that the other woman wore a look of displeasure, her long brows drawn together as she gazed out, presumably seeing the white portico, its pediment painted in gay polychrome, that would rise from the site some months hence.

"What is it?" Helena asked.

"I question," Delia said heavily, "our design."

"But... I thought you were very pleased with Miss Montague's work."

"Oh, absolutely, the fault's not with Miss Montague, I fear it may be with me."

"What do you mean?"

"Perhaps it's too fanciful, this idea of confecting all these styles—a Greek temple with Byzantine ornament, Roman gardens with Moorish mosaics... I had thought there would be something joyful about bringing them all together—under Miss Montague's classical discipline—but now I can't get it all to sit right in my head. Suppose it just looks like... a dessert."

"A dessert!"

"Or a pageant. Something trivial, affected. I mean... something where visitors would come and sniff about and then satisfy themselves by saying... 'Looks like women's work.'"

Helena was startled and discomfited. Her graceful, broad-shouldered aunt always seemed to operate entirely under her own power, like a galleon blown by winds that no one else could summon. She seemed to navigate with thoughtless ease around objection and opposition. She might make joking reference to difficulties she had encountered as a woman who lived alone, worked alone, and traveled alone; or she might dissect them with Helena for practical purposes. But never before had she expressed herself so, well, gloomily.

Worried, Helena looked up at her aunt, and found that Delia was looking at her somberly. All of a sudden, she realized that Delia had shared this with her, at least in part, as a form of confidence: *You may think I am unassailable,* her aunt's look said, *but I, too, have my doubts; and it's time you began to bear that in mind.*

Overcome with affection, Helena turned to her aunt and embraced her tightly, not caring what the workmen thought. When she released her, she said fondly, "But don't you always tell me that Thessaloniki is the best of all the Greek cities?"

"Dear Saloniki," Delia said slowly, smiling; she might have been addressing Helena as such. "Yes, taken from the Byzantines by the Ottomans, and then by the Greeks again. Every church a mosque, and every mosque a church. Yes, it's at the borders of things that life, and art, get interesting... though

I wish the Turks would give up their latest sally; poor Thessaloniki's people and streets deserve at least another century's rest."

Helena watched anxiously to see if her attempt to distract, or redirect, her aunt had succeeded.

"As usual, my dear," Aunt Delia continued, "you are right." (Helena thought this was too much credit.) "Though it's one thing for the broad hand of history to reconfigure a multitude of peoples and places, and another for one woman, full of foibles and conceits, to attempt the same."

"I'd think that your hand is rather much kinder," Helena put in, still thinking of the Turkish war, which had overtaken the Macedonian region only months after the Great War itself, delivering yet more strife.

"Well, who's to say," Aunt Delia said, and her voice regained some of its customary vigor. "Perhaps I've only been looking too closely at plans, and not trusting myself to feel the spirit of the fragments of history we've summoned across the sea to us, here on the western shore... Perhaps I ought to call on Andros again." This was a Greek friend of Delia's, a diplomat and fellow collector. "And when the museum is done, we shall have to invite some Turkish delegates, too, and Arabs; and they shall have the final say as to my taste."

And since it was Delia, Helena knew that this would, in fact, take place.

Aunt Delia touched her shoulder, smiling, and the two women proceeded on their tour about the site.

* * *

After they had clambered about the foundations and Aunt Delia had questioned the foreman on a number of particulars, an hour had passed. Delia and Helena thanked the crew, patted the dust off their skirts, and retired to be driven back for a late lunch. Helena took it as a mark of Delia's recovered spirits that she chatted animatedly with her driver, Richard, nearly the entire while back to the city, despite the dry hot wind. But it dampened *her* spirits when Richard asked if Miss Helena hadn't yet found a nice Western boy, or three, to take back with her to Philadelphia.

Helena's answering laughter was forced and too bright, and Richard hurried the conversation onward. Helena lapsed into silence, staring at the scrub-covered hills.

At an airy restaurant in Los Angeles, they refreshed themselves on celery hearts, broiled chicken, and creamed mushrooms, and Aunt Delia told Helena about what it had been like when she had first started collecting art and artifacts. She had often been barred from auctions and sales, she said, and had had to pester gentleman friends into accompanying or even standing in for her. "But if they started thinking that they were entitled to bring their own opinions into it," Delia confided with relish, "I dropped them. I couldn't bear to have some wet-behind-the-ears Yale 'man' lecture me about *chiaroscuro*." Helena laughed, delighted.

As they concluded with orange ices, Helena grew quiet again, and could sense her aunt's inquisitive gaze on her.

She thought of the moment at the museum site when her aunt had finally confided a thread of doubt, however thin, to her. Might she presume...?

"Aunt Delia?" she said carefully. She ran her spoon around the inside of her nearly empty dish.

"Yes, dear?"

"May I ask you an awfully personal question?"

"You may."

"All of your friends... the ones who helped you at auctions or, or, took you to villas and things..."

"Yes?"

"Surely some of them... liked you quite a lot, if you know what I mean."

"I'm sure some did." Aunt Delia smiled.

"Aunt Delia, what I mean is... how did you decide not to get married?" Helena's cheeks heated. "Well, maybe you didn't decide, maybe it just... happened, but..."

Aunt Delia touched her hand reassuringly, then let out a little sigh. "As a matter of fact," she said, "I did decide, very distinctly, that I didn't want to get married."

Helena fixed her gaze on her. Her heartbeat came fast.

"Here, I'll tell you the story, and you can judge my reasoning for yourself. Let's see. I had just turned eighteen years old, if you can believe that I ever was such an age. I was taken on my first voyage abroad, the summer that I was done with finishing school. Paris, Lisbon, and then—I could hardly believe my luck—Morocco. It was Father, Mother, myself, and your father." Helena's father was Delia's elder brother. "Our little sister had been left at home because she was too young; she was terribly disappointed.

"In Morocco, we were to see Casablanca, then Marrakech. We had a guide, a young local man named Haddaoui. He must have been about twenty-two. He was very serious and spoke beautiful English, French, Spanish, and of course Arabic and Berber. You see where I am going with this, perhaps.

"I instantly thought that he was the most interesting and wise person I had ever met, although he was careful to say very little about himself. We did learn that his mother was widowed, and he had three little sisters; you could see that he was very fond of them. One could guess that almost all the money that he made would have gone toward them.

"I said next to nothing to him, myself; Father did almost all of the talking. But at night I would lie awake and listen to the city and think about how different this young man's life was from mine, and how much more of consequence he must have seen than me—trade and colonization and uprisings, but also, simply, the basic facts of life. The death of his father, hunger, uncertainty. Death faces us all, of course, but people like you and I, we know so little of the kind of basic necessity that most of the world is shaped by."

Helena had gripped her hands together tightly in her lap, listening.

"I felt that this kind of experience of reality," Aunt Delia went on, "separated him from me. We often think of rich young people as having a glow about them. In this case, I felt that it was the opposite: that I was utterly dull and insubstantial, silly and empty, while Haddaoui had a kind of mantle of saintliness on him. A 'saint of the world,' was the phrase I began to repeat to myself.

"Since then, I've had many hours and years to think about how youthful and silly all those notions were, themselves. Haddaoui was a person, as are you and I; he was not a saint, even though I thought he was clever and wise enough to be anything he wanted to be—a professor, a diplomat.

"Nonetheless, my ideas had some real consequences. Chiefly, I decided that since it was inconceivable that I would ever be allowed to marry Haddaoui, I would never get married at all."

And here Delia stopped. She sat back to take a drink of water, watching Helena's expression closely.

Helena clasped and unclasped her hands. "Truly?" she said finally. "That's why?"

"That's why," Aunt Delia said, with a slight smile.

Helena couldn't get ahold of her thoughts. *All these years,* she thought, *because of an Arab boy she met once... a boy she hardly spoke to...*

"There is a post-script to this story," Aunt Delia added, after a little silence.

"Yes?" Helena said breathlessly.

"I managed to find Haddaoui again, decades later. He had a shop in the medina in Marrakech. He had married and had two children. He was plumper, and it suited him; he was also much less serious. He remembered me, just barely. I didn't try to press him much on it, anyway. I bought some things from him, chatted about his children, and went on my way."

Again, Helena was lost for words, but now she found that she had tears in her eyes.

"Oh, now," Aunt Delia said gently.

Swiping at her eyes with her napkin helped Helena to recollect her thoughts. "All that time," she said softly to Aunt Delia, "how did you keep your resolve? Didn't you ever question it?"

"Of course I did," said Delia. "But what I found also was that it was like putting on a new dress that you think at first won't suit you at all—on a whim you toss it on, but once you have, you find that it fits you better than you might ever have imagined. Pretty soon, you can't imagine wearing anything else.

"The longer I went on, the more I saw the advantages of my choice. It helped, of course, that I had never been the beauty of the family—if I wanted to hang back all the time, that was unremarkable. But altogether, though I'm sure there are things that might have been easier in my life, had I chosen to have a man in it—there are a great many things that went my way, and my way only, because I didn't." And here Delia smiled, deeply and warmly, her large, sleepy grey eyes glowing with contentment.

"It's not an advantage that's available to women of all walks of life, of course. But I am glad that I saw a chance for myself—even if that's not how I was thinking of it, at the time that I met Haddaoui. And I'm glad that I took it."

Helena gazed at her for a while longer, and then away. She looked in a daze at the restaurant around them, once again growing aware of the clink of cutlery, the urbane chatter, the indifferent gilt-framed paintings of chrysanthemums. Again she was without words.

With gentle humor, Delia said, "I do hope you hadn't been hoping for a lesson. I can offer those in history, but not in life. In life, I have always been drawn to compelling choices, not sensible ones."

Helena still found it difficult to smile in response. After another moment, she shook herself, thanked Aunt Delia for sharing her story, apologized for her silence, and suggested that they might return home.

As they settled themselves in the car, Richard whistling in the front seat, Helena once again rested her head against Delia's shoulder. Delia caressed her hair and said softly, "Are you so very unhappy, my Helena?"

Once again, Helena said nothing. She thought of sun and blue shadows slanting in a medina; she thought of Delia, alone, because of love.

* * *

"Do *you* know what your mother's up to?" Helena demanded of Michael, *sotto voce*. After Mrs. Byrne had asked her to tea, Helena had retaliated, as it were, by inquiring whether she might see Michael the same day, too. Mrs. Byrne had agreed: Helena might call on him the hour before tea, while Mrs. Byrne concluded a philanthropic discussion.

"I haven't a clue," Michael replied. With some effort, he dragged his linked hands over to one side of his lap, so that he could lean on one of his armrests. His dark, waving hair was slightly disarranged today; Helena wished she could set it right, though she considered that it made him look a bit rakish, especially as they were surrounded by a tropical profusion of ferns and trees. They were sitting today in the little conservatory beyond the gallery. The air was filled with a moist, mineral scent, and four rosy-gray finches with vivid red beaks hopped and chattered to one another inside a lofty cage by the window. "I don't even know how to begin speculating," Michael continued. "With Mother, it could be nothing or anything. And she's... selective about what she tells me, you know, even if I can usually find out more from the servants."

"If it were *nothing*, surely she could have told me at the party... Did the servants know anything this time?" Helena cast a glance at Karl, who, as usual, had withdrawn as far as he could without getting all the way clear of eyeshot; he occupied himself with letters in the gallery. (She thought that she and Michael had gotten themselves into a damnable stalemate: because she had never yet surrendered her pride enough to ask Karl to simply leave them alone, neither had Michael, in deference to her apparent sensibilities.)

"Mother likes to be informed," Michael said. "Even if she wanted to chat about something small—ask after someone with whom she wants to be connected back East, say—perhaps your reaction would be more informative in isolation than at a party."

"This is really not reassuring, Michael. But what did the servants say?"

"Oh, right. On this account, nothing, I'm afraid to say. I can promise they were very apologetic. They like you, you know."

Gloomily, Helena considered her report to her parents: *Well, no, I didn't like any of the nice boys, and I made sure they didn't like me, either. But the Byrne family servants, you might ask* them *for a reference for me.*

She shook her head with a little exhalation of breath, pushed her hair back, and addressed Michael: "I'm sorry, I'll leave it be. I don't mean to waste your time with hand-wringing. But I won't be able to concentrate enough to carry a conversation, now. You'll need to tell me a story."

He smiled. "What sort of story?"

"Tell me... tell me how you were educated." She had been wondering about it for some time.

"Hmm. Is that a story?"

"It is, to me." They shared a smile, until Helena began to feel that she was being pulled too deep. She glanced away, as if one of the finches had caught her eye.

When she looked back, she found that Michael's elbow had slipped off his armrest, so that he had slumped down over his lap, shaking; she waited until he was able to lift himself up again, rolling his head back against the seat.

"Well," he said, licking his lips, "I had a tutor named Jack Durrey. Wonderful chap. When I was seven, he started coming five days a week, and he kept on doing that till I turned eighteen. When I was small, I used to cry at the end of the day when he left." Helena's heart clenched. "Bit of an odd duck, but I only realized that from how my family and the servants

—even Karl, yes, unflappable Karl—used to react to things he did. I expect he would have gotten along well with your Aunt Delia.

"When I got older, I was able to piece together that he'd been studying up to be a professor of languages—he'd even done work at Oxford—but he'd disgraced himself somehow and got 'sent down,' as they say. He drifted around for a bit after that, until my mother heard of him and offered him a nice salary as a private tutor, if he could be discreet." Michael paused. "Mother had to argue with Father to do it, you know. Father couldn't see what the point was if I was just going to 'sit around my whole life.'" Helena pressed her lips together. "But Mother argued with him until she had to shout that she had brought money of her own to the marriage, and if she had to, she would use that to educate her son as she pleased... I wasn't present for any of this, of course. Betty the housekeeper told me, when I was much older."

Michael watched Helena's reaction closely for a moment, then continued in a lighter tone. "But anyway, as I was saying, he was eccentric. When I first met him, I had met so few outside people that I could hardly understand where he came from, let alone what he was talking about. He started out by addressing me as if I were a graduate student, you see." Helena gave a delighted laugh, and Michael grinned; his head tilted over towards one shoulder. "But he quickly caught on to what he needed to do to get through to me; and I caught on to him.

"I think it was hard for him to remember that other people were people, and not just... places where he could get more ideas, or receptacles where he could swirl his about. But I think that in a way, it made him peculiarly suited to be my tutor, because he didn't see me as being significantly more strange or startling than any other person. And of course it excited him tremendously when it turned out that I liked learning, a lot. I liked nothing better than hearing his ideas, and trying out some of my own." Michael paused to push himself up slowly with his legs, carefully righting his head as he did.

"And he was capable of paying attention, in his way. He was the first one who noticed that I could actually move my legs in a way that might let me walk a bit. When he first pointed it out, and said that I ought to practice, Mother was furious. I think it was with herself, because she hadn't thought about it that way before. For Jack, it was simple: if you saw something interesting that could be tried, then you should try it."

Michael paused, looking off to one side and smiling. "What else? I suppose I should say that he wasn't just a book-scholar. He also liked to take me out on little rambles; he would carry me on his back and help me learn different kinds of lizards—minerals—that sort of thing. You know I don't often get to go about and touch things. It was wonderful."

He rolled his head back towards Helena again, and said, "All in all, the very least I can say is—he was a grand teacher, and I miss him. I'm lucky that Mother fought for him."

Helena rubbed one hand over the back of the other, picturing the figure of a scarecrow scholar—she pictured him with poky ginger hair, spectacles, and a flapping coat—scrambling about a dry gully. A lanky boy clung to his back; the scholar helped him to stretch out one wavering hand to touch a pitted shelf of sandstone.

"Michael," she said after a moment, "you protested, but that was a *beautiful* story. Thank you. When did you last hear from him?"

"We exchange letters sometimes, actually. He's been traveling and working in Europe for a while now. The last letter I got from him came from Geneva."

With a wooden dowel held in his mouth, Michael could type a bit on a typewriter, but it was exhausting for him; Helena knew that to write letters of any length, he often dictated to Karl. And of course any number of others in the household, chiefly Mrs. Byrne, might handle the letters before they were sealed and posted. She wondered how frank Michael had ever dared to be in his correspondence.

"He's been working on a number of scholarly endeavors with a Frenchman," Michael was saying, smiling to himself. "They seem quite pleased with each other."

Something about his tone touched off a reaction in Helena; she felt it like a white spark leaping from a struck flint. She glanced swiftly in Karl's direction; his head was bent assiduously over his papers. Before she could question herself, she stood up from her chair and seized the front of each of Michael's armrests, stepping backwards and drawing him towards herself at the same time, until they were no longer within Karl's view, sheltering within the conservatory.

Michael jerked with surprise, his eyes widening and meeting

hers before he collapsed forward over his lap, catching himself on his forearms.

When he looked up again, she was kneeling in front of him, and reached out her hands to cup his face, steadying it as he looked at her in startlement, his lips parted.

Helena leaned forward and kissed him for a long time.

When they parted, there was a furrow between his brows. "I've missed you," he said, his voice very low. His head twisted to one side. She moved her hands to stroke his hair gently, finally smoothing it, as he trembled and jerked under her touch. She heard him exhale.

"I'm sorry," she said after a pause. *I'm sorry, I'm sorry, I'm sorry.* Part of her felt as if she were already on the train, leaving. She didn't know what else to say. She leaned until she could rest her brow against his shoulder, not caring how it might move.

They stayed like this for some time. Once, Karl cleared his throat softly in the gallery, and they both chose to ignore it.

Finally Michael pushed himself up straighter in his wheelchair, clearing his own throat. He looked in the direction of the caged finches. "Will you help me...?" he said.

She knew what he meant, and stood back to watch as he pulled himself closer to the cage with his feet. When he was situated before it, she reached out to unlatch the cage door, then caught Michael's left wrist as he lifted it with great effort toward the open door. Jolts ran through the rest of his body as he fought to control his left hand, but together, they were able to bring his hand close to the finch that had hopped over to investigate. Carefully Helena steadied his hand as the delicate bird edged onto Michael's fingers, uttering bright chirps and constantly glancing about with its round black eyes.

Like this, Michael watched the bird explore his hand, hopping about nimbly as his fingers curled and uncurled of their own volition. His face was pensive, almost stern. Helena held his wrist, feeling the warmth of his skin and watching him in silence until, finally, Karl came to fetch her away.

* * *

Mrs. Byrne plied her with finger sandwiches, cakes, berries with whipped cream, hot Ceylon tea. Helena sipped her tea and tried to not to smile too much or too little. Mrs. Byrne quizzed her about her father's business, the De Vries family summer house, the progress on the construction of Delia's museum.

Dwelling on this last topic, Mrs. Byrne remarked, "Your aunt recently taught me the notion of the *hortus conclusus*."

Mrs. Byrne's pale gaze looked expectant; Helena tried not to shift uncomfortably. "Yes, the enclosed garden," she replied. "Were you discussing the plans for the museum grounds?"

"Well, more generally she was telling me about the line of descent of this notion—the ancestry of the *hortus conclusus*..." She lifted her eyebrows at Helena, inviting her to go on.

"The gardens of a Roman villa," Helena said, feeling unpleasantly as if she were reciting a lesson for an exacting teacher, "then the walled gardens of Persia, and North Africa

—and then the medieval cloistered garden, in the monasteries of Europe... Is this what you mean?"

"Yes, that's it. All laid out along the same lines, offering respite from the rigors of the world. A cool sunny courtyard with lemons, quinces, rosemary, and playing water... I think this is an apt metaphor for Delia's museum: a treasure-box offering a moment of delight and refreshment, before one goes out again to all the dust and commotion." Just as Helena was beginning to grow uncomfortable with this uncharacteristic display of lyricism, Mrs. Byrne changed her tone again. "Your modesty as to your learning is commendable, Miss De Vries. By now I've seen you're almost as much an expert as your aunt, even if you don't like to show it." *Not to* you, Helena thought scathingly, her conversations with Michael flashing back into her mind. "It's true you went to college in New York? For history?"

"Yes," said Helena, very carefully, "it was my privilege to complete a degree."

"An admirable display of persistence," Mrs. Byrne offered.

Helena managed a small smile. "Thank you. There were challenges, it's true."

"Oh yes," Mrs. Byrne said smoothly, "because you almost got married, instead."

Helena was silent. Her cheeks felt very cold.

Mrs. Byrne took a sip of her tea. She watched Helena levelly, letting the silence stretch on.

Helena felt simultaneously numbed and enraged: *How dare she humiliate me like this—and how dare she do it over something that matters so little to me now?* The engagement, whatever feelings she had once had about it—they all seemed now like luggage that had been discarded from a wagon train, left hundreds of miles behind, scattered and dust-choked. What was real, what was alive in her life, had nothing to do with the events of almost two years ago.

She stared back at Mrs. Byrne, at her smooth face and smooth hair, around which the tension in the room seemed to coalesce, like the center of a whirlpool.

"Miss De Vries," Mrs. Byrne said finally, "having been indelicate just now, I am afraid I am going to continue to pursue that line of inquiry. This is because I wish to speak to you of something that I believe is of pressing interest to us both. What I mean is: it seems to me that you're very fond of my son."

Helena felt the flush spring up almost painfully in her cheeks. The numbness broke. "Your son..." she said in a low voice. She gripped her skirt in one hand, clenching the fabric tight.

"Yes, I mean that I cannot mistake the special affection that exists between you... and Lewis."

Helena was speechless. She stared at Mrs. Byrne, her mouth open. She began to say something, realized that she didn't even know what she wanted to say, and glanced aside, her cheeks still burning, her mind producing only hectic fragments of nonsense. She had to restrain a hysterical laugh.

By the time she had looked up again at Mrs. Byrne and forcibly wiped any expression—she thought—from her face, Mrs. Byrne was watching her with a kind of cool fascination.

There was a subtle but unmistakable lift of amusement to the corners of her mouth.

She knows, Helena thought, *and she has known all along. How could we have ever, ever thought she would not know?*

"Your son," Helena repeated finally. She firmed her mouth and drew herself up in her seat; she even reached out a hand to lift her cup of tea, and was pleased when it did not tremble. But when she thought to speak, she found she could only shake her head mutely at Mrs. Byrne. Hysterical laughter still threatened.

Mrs. Byrne exhaled, folding her hands together on the table-top, and turning her face slightly to one side, as if abashed, though her expression didn't change at all. "Yes, that was a test, if a very poor one. I know you're fond of Lewis—it's hard not to be—but anyone with an ounce of sensibility couldn't imag-ine any real depth of feeling developing between you two.

"But so. What of *Michael*?" And Mrs. Byrne turned her face fully toward Helena again, as if wanting to see the impact of the name.

"What," said Helena, "do you want me to say?" And she was proud of how cold her voice was.

"As little as you want," Mrs. Byrne replied, "Your faces speak enough, whenever you're together. I have no intention of interrogating you further on the subject. In fact, if it pleases you, you needn't speak now, except to tell me what you think of a certain proposition that I would like to share with you."

"How generous," Helena couldn't help saying.

"You think I'm very cold," Mrs. Byrne said, "I know that.

I'm not going to try to disabuse you of that. I want to speak to you about things that are important to me, and I think it best to do so in the most straightforward manner possible. I will do so because I have seen enough to trust that you are intelligent, feeling—and *discreet.*"

Watching Mrs. Byrne closely, weighing the intensity of her gaze, Helena was gradually realizing that there was, in fact, a kind of distant, pained vulnerability underlying the almost contemptuous directness of the other woman's approach. Mrs. Byrne was operating under so much tension that—it was just as she had said—she could only manage to be direct. A subtler, more intricate approach would have been too taxing to sustain. Helena pushed this dim apprehension aside, to revisit later.

She met Mrs. Byrne's eyes squarely and gave her a deliberate nod. She found that, despite her discomfiture, her keenly struck pride, a vivid sprout of curiosity had risen up within her.

Mrs. Byrne exhaled through her nose. "Well. I'm going to speak to you first of Lewis, and I promise this time that I'm not presenting you with a decoy, though it may seem beside the point to begin with."

"I see," said Helena. "Well, please do continue." And she forced herself to settle back into her chair after a sip of tea.

"What do you know," Mrs. Byrne asked, "of Mr. Plainsborough?"

"Mr. *Plainsborough?*" Helena said, once again feeling, despite Mrs. Byrne's promise, that she had been taken in by a bait and switch. It took her a moment to even recall who Mrs. Byrne meant: Lewis Byrne's tall, strange college friend.

"Yes. *Please*. What do you know of him? Or what do you think of him?" And Mrs. Byrne leaned forward a fraction of an inch, watching Helena intently.

Bewildered, Helena cast about. "He practices law. He went to college with Lewis. He's from Chicago, but he doesn't miss it." She felt she was embarrassing herself with the banality of these remarks, but John Daniel Plainsborough was hardly a revealing conversant, and she was hardly motivated to draw him out.

"Anything else?"

What *was* it she was expecting to hear? Helena tried to sharpen the point of her recollections. Was Mrs. Byrne hoping for more personal judgments? "I find him strange; certainly aloof, and perhaps a bit cruel. I don't know why Lewis likes him so much," she concluded, hoping that this blunter assessment would satisfy Mrs. Byrne's searching look.

But when Mrs. Byrne leaned back again, she looked, if anything, disappointed. "I hadn't counted," she said, "on your being so detached from society talk. Well, I suppose that reflects well on you."

Helena pushed out a hard breath. What was to stop her from simply getting up and leaving? She couldn't: there was the promise that these slights and pushes would, eventually, resolve in something to do with Michael.

"I asked you about Mr. Plainsborough," Mrs. Byrne said,

"hoping you might already know what I am about to tell you." *So she wouldn't have to say it herself?* Helena wondered.

Mrs. Byrne tapped the index finger of one outspread hand on the table a few times before proceeding. "What I want you to understand is that Lewis and Mr. Plainsborough... have a special relationship." She paused, her face especially severe. Then she said, "Do you know what it is that I am talking about?"

Helena blinked and looked aside. Her already battered brain was whirling with half-formed thoughts; for a moment her thoughts broke away so completely to Michael, as if seeking relief, that she had to force herself to remember what Mrs. Byrne was trying to bring her to understand.

She thought. She thought about the bizarre approximation of flirtation with which Mr. Plainsborough had first approached her; she thought about how he had seemed to settle back, dismissing her, once he had satisfied himself that she was not interested in rising to the bait. She thought about the faint air of menace that he exuded whenever he trailed Lewis at a party; she had thought of it before as *watchful*, but now the word that came to mind was... *jealous*.

She thought, too, about a certain tone of complicity that occasionally entered the conversation when Lewis was being discussed by society sophisticates. She had taken it as condescension towards his puppyishness, but...

She thought of a look that she had once intercepted between Lewis and Mr. Plainsborough. She thought of the sudden, ferocious heat that Mr. Plainsborough had turned on her when he had realized that she was watching.

She thought of Mrs. Byrne saying, *Your faces speak enough, whenever you're together.*

"Oh," she said finally. "*Oh.*" She put a hand to her mouth.

For the first time since Helena had known her, Mrs. Byrne looked tired. "So you've come to it after all."

"I... I think I have," Helena said. The desire to get up, to run away, rose up in her. This was too much, too much for one conversation. How much further could Mrs. Byrne push her? She rested her hands around her cup of tea, seeking the solidity of a familiar object; the tea had gone cold by now.

"Shall I go on?" Mrs. Byrne said, her voice this time surprisingly gentle.

Helena breathed. "Yes," she said.

"Miss De Vries," Mrs. Byrne said, "I am like any other mother. I want Lewis to retain a secure position in society; if possible, to rise, even. With matters as they are, he is vulnerable. I am not naïve enough to think that I can simply order him to set aside his friendship with Mr. Plainsborough and afterwards expect things to be cut off cleanly and entirely—no matter what consequences I threatened.

"He, also, realizes his vulnerability, on some level—I think. But he's too light at heart to pursue the work of shoring up his reputation with any degree of seriousness. Or he believes that he is so generally liked that it would buffer him from any real incident, should something arise. Or both.

"I am not one to trust in the persistence of sheer likability under duress." She paused to let Helena digest this, to silently signal her understanding. "And—if we were to reach the point of testing that persistence, that means that matters would have risen to the level of my husband's notice. If you think I am cold—you must understand that my husband would be more than cold, were everything to come clear to him. He would be brutal." Mrs. Byrne said this matter-of-factly.

Helena stroked her thumbs nervously over the rim of her cup, and said softly, "I understand." Her mind flitted to the elder brother of a college friend, who had been disowned after he had been excessively public in pursuing an unsuitable woman. His father had merely sent a letter; the two had never spoken again.

Mrs. Byrne drew herself up in her seat. "Miss De Vries, I will lay all the pieces before you. Your parents sent you here to be a companion and able assistant to your aunt, yes, but also to meet young men of appropriate wealth and stature. My son Lewis needs a conventional household—a conventional *marriage*.

"Lewis has also made it clear, in word and in deed, that he would like nothing so much as to continue living like the boy he is at heart. He wants the people whom he loves to always be around him—and you know that his love includes Michael, very deeply."

Against her will, the name once again pulled at Helena; it quickened her heart. She felt, for a moment, as if he were watching her.

"Let us entertain the possibility," Mrs. Byrne suggested,

"that Lewis were to be married, to someone amiable, someone understanding. He would have his own house, not just a little bachelor flat in the city. To a great extent—given that amiability, that understanding—he could maintain his own ways. So might the other person in that marriage. And so who is to say that that house, and those ways, could not also contain—a certain beloved brother." She said these last words with great deliberation.

"Is that," Helena said quietly, "your idea of a 'conventional household'?"

Mrs. Byrne's expression in response was so strained that Helena actually regretted her sarcasm. She compressed her lips, thinking of the immense vulnerability, the exquisitely sensitive confidence that this proud woman was placing in her hands.

And yet—it was fantastical, what Mrs. Byrne was suggesting. Such a thing simply couldn't be sustained. Her mind staggered between emergencies and humiliations, imagining all the ways it could fall apart, all the ways somcone—*some-ones*—in such a situation could be caught out.

And yet again—creeping back into her mind came all the society tales, the husbands who kept a mistress for every city visited, the wives with sweethearts at their call. Amicable arrangements, well-negotiated accords. How much could be forgiven, overlooked, elided, if only one had a pretty wife to point to, a placid husband... and better yet, a tidy string of children.

But it was all dangerous, so dangerous...

Here a cold suggestion, sudden, arresting, came into her head for the first time: what if her mind was rebelling not because the thing was impossible, but because she *wished* it to be impossible?

What if *she didn't really love Michael?* Not enough, not truly—no matter how lost and tormented she thought herself, perhaps it was all conceit, self-delusion, playing on the vulnerabilities of a profoundly isolated man.

Delia had rejected marriage altogether because of love for one man. Here Helena was being offered marriage, comfort, and love, all in one tidy envelope, a poisonous *billet-doux*. If she could not bring herself to reach towards it, was it because she was, after all, a coward, a false lover?

Here her train of thought, barely sustained, broke apart into a shower of painful fragments.

When she looked back up at Mrs. Byrne, all she could do at first was shake her head.

After another moment, she said with difficulty, "Mrs. Byrne, I understand what it is you are suggesting. I... appreciate the confidence you have placed in me. But I will have to consider this... proposal... at greater length. Much greater length."

"As you should," Mrs. Byrne said. Here she hesitated. Then, with the air of relinquishing one last confidence, she said, "I have two impossible sons. I care for them both greatly. I hope that if nothing else, you come away from this conversation knowing that to be true." And her smile was pained.

Helena imagined that the look she gave in return could only have been similar.

They rose almost simultaneously; Mrs. Byrne abruptly rang for the maid to come and take away the tea things. She saw Helena to the door, and they parted almost wordlessly.

* * *

To add insult to injury, when Helena exited the mansion, she found that waiting on the drive below was not only Delia's car, but also three riders astride taut, slender horses. They cast harsh black shadows on the drive. Two of the riders were brown-haired, round-cheeked sisters, faintly known to her, and daringly outfitted in jodhpurs. The third rider was Winston Byrne, Michael's identical twin.

Helena froze.

The riders were chatting in the sun, apparently conferring as to the direction of their ride: Winston was gesturing animatedly, egging the sisters on, while they shook their heads, laughing. When he noticed Helena appearing on the steps above them, he paused, squinting up at her. She flinched back from the touch of his gaze, feeling a sick lurch as if she had entered into a nightmare.

She could not escape the *wrongness* of his resemblance to Michael. The shape of his nose, the darkness of his narrowed eyes, the lines on either side of his mouth, the way his face shifted between expressions: all of it was so uncannily specific. She thought of the Germanic legend of the *doppelgänger*, the dark double, who brings his original's death when finally met.

But Winston's shoulders and thighs were thick with muscle;

he sat astride his horse with easy fluidity as it fidgeted nervously beneath him. There was a curl to his upper lip that spoke of habitual self-regard. He was not, after all, Michael's double.

With bitterness, she watched him, expressionless. She wondered what it would have been like to go riding with Michael —to go walking with him, even, to simply walk together into the long California dusk.

Looking slightly quizzical, Winston Byrne smiled with one side of his mouth and raised a hand in greeting, before urging his horse into a trot away from the mansion. She didn't respond, still staring; the sisters followed him more slowly, peering curiously over their shoulders at Helena before picking up speed.

As the sound of their hoofbeats faded, Helena pressed her fingertips to her temples. She felt as if she hadn't remembered to breathe for some time. She could see Richard, Delia's driver, watching her from the car below, and hastily transformed the gesture to seem as if she were rearranging her hair under her cloche.

She felt the pressure of tears threatening. She wished she could run back into the house and find Michael.

Forcibly, she pushed the thought away.

She told herself to walk down the steps, to smile gratefully when Richard opened the door for her. As he started the engine, she surprised him by immediately asking after his wife, his two children; for the remainder of the drive back to Aunt Delia's, he maintained a steady stream of genial chatter, and Helena relaxed back into it. She luxuriated in the solidity, the normalcy of this man: the simplicity of his goodwill, his pride in his family, his hopes that they would learn trades and marry happily.

But at the end of the drive, the sound of Mrs. Byrne's voice came back to her: *I am like any other mother. ... I have two impossible sons.* The memory of the phrase drove a dart into her breast, and she flinched around its sting.

With apologies, she told Delia that the drive had given her a headache, and she retired at once to her bedroom, drawing the curtains. Not even bothering to undress, she lay back in bed and stared at the ceiling, her eyes dry and unseeing.

* * *

After a time, she found she had closed her eyes; had she slept without realizing it? She opened her eyes again.

She felt as if she were running a fever, but when she put the back of her hand to her forehead, it was merely warm. She bit out an exasperated exclamation. Was it disappointment because she didn't have a real excuse to be in bed in the middle of the afternoon? Or was it a more childish, romantic dissatisfaction—because she wanted her body to express the bewilderment and distress that roiled her brain?

She rolled over and buried her face in her pillow, holding her breath. A memory was pressing into her mind; she resisted it. Finally she exhaled. As her hot breath pushed into the pillow, she let the memory color her mind once more.

She remembered an afternoon in late July, another afternoon at the Byrne mansion. Delia was meeting with Mrs. Byrne to discuss the garden lecture, and afterwards the two planned to take dinner together with a covey of potential donors. After a brief consultation on some details of the ceramics to be presented at the lecture, Helena had been released. She might enjoy the music room, Mrs. Byrne suggested, or go riding, or, if she pleased, call upon Michael. (Thinking back now, Helena racked her memory, trying to recall if there had been any hint of complicity in Mrs. Byrne's looks, her tone. But it was impossible to retrieve the details without their being wholly tinted by the conversation of today.)

Helena had smiled and departed, not too hastily, for the east wing.

In the gallery, Michael's gallery: the same sunlight, the same smell of warm wood and books, the same brilliant smile when he looked up from his newspapers and saw her. Happiness fluttered up in her chest.

"But where's Karl?" she said, looking about curiously; she almost never saw Michael without his manservant.

Michael's head had briefly fallen towards his chest. As he worked to lift it again, he said, a little muffled, "His youngest sister is getting married this Sunday. We've given him the week off."

"That's wonderful!" she exclaimed. "What do you know about his sister?"

"I'll tell you all about her," Michael offered, "if you take me down to the garden."

Helena blinked at him. She put her hands together uncertainly; she felt as if she had been asked to do something she wasn't allowed. But why should it be forbidden? It was simply unprecedented, because Karl was always there to help. But then the thought followed: it was forbidden because she no longer allowed herself to be alone with Michael.

Michael was looking at her inquisitively now, watching her hesitate.

Before the moment could go on too long, she pushed aside her confusion and smiled. "Yes, let's do that."

He smiled widely and pushed himself back from the table with his feet, and she approached to begin steering his wheelchair towards the elevator at the back of the wing.

As he chatted about Karl's sister—she was a schoolteacher, living about half a day's travel north; her husband-to-be was a shopkeeper—Helena noted that Michael's body was more relaxed than usual that day. His arms lay softly in his lap, palms up, only occasionally lifting to tap against each other briefly, rather than constantly writhing. She watched his gently curled hands, and then the back of his neck, resisting the urge to stroke it, or kiss it. The urge grew so strong that she lost track of what he was saying, simply hearing the sound of his voice, feeling the warmth of his presence.

When they reached the elevator, she had to give her head a little shake to clear it. She reached out to push the call button. As the elevator car hummed into motion below them, she realized that Michael had twisted around to look up at her—always an awkward position for him to maintain. "I'm sorry," she said ruefully, "I was miles away just then. But—Camilla sounds just as sharp and steady as Karl. They're a good family... Her fiancé is a lucky man."

"Hm," was all Michael said, giving a brief, warm smile, before collapsing forward again. She pushed his chair into the elevator. Its ostensible use was for servants to move about furniture and so on, but of course it was Michael's means of access onto the paths that circled the grounds of the Byrne mansion. She knew that someone—usually Karl, but sometimes Lewis, and very occasionally Mrs. Byrne herself—took him out into the gardens every day. He could also operate the elevator himself, with a little difficulty given his hands, but seemed to prefer to have company when going outdoors.

They took the ride down together in silence. Helena had clasped her hands behind her back, but just before the elevator doors opened again, she raised one to touch it to the back of Michael's neck, lightly caressing. His whole body jerked in reaction, but he said nothing; nor did he turn to look at her again. She replaced her hands on the push-bar of his chair, and they went out into the insect song and dappled shade of the gardens.

Their silence persisted, but it was not uncomfortable, Helena thought. For once, her mind seemed to have retreated; she looked about dreamily, registering patterns of light and shadow and color. Unless Michael indicated a preference, she chose paths at random, meandering among silvery olive trees and fragrant banks of rosemary and lavender, vast terracotta urns of oleander, the occasional sculpture of a graceful nymph or a swan with wings outspread. Sparrows hopped in the undergrowth. One of Michael's forearms had lifted slightly off his lap, the fingers of that hand slowly opening and closing; she watched the familiar gesture from one corner of her eye.

Other than Delia, there were no other guests at the house that day, and she knew the groundskeepers had long since completed their daily rounds, which began not much after dawn. They were alone in the gardens.

Along a tall alley of boxwoods, overhung by arching boughs of live oak, Helena paused at a particularly inviting turning: an entrance into what seemed a little enclosure of hedges, with the sound of running water within. On either side of the entrance stood a lemon tree hung with glowing fruit. Michael lifted one shaking hand and managed to brush his knuckles against the pebbly rind of one lemon, before his hand dropped back into his lap. Helena imagined that the warmth of his touch released a curl of citrus scent into the air.

When he didn't make a further gesture, she pushed his chair through the entrance into the hedges, curious. There, the boxwoods formed a small, circular enclosure, more than head-high, like the heart of a hedge maze. Directly across from the entrance, there was a simple fountain set into a rock wall: a thin stream of water emerged from a narrow brass pipe, trickling several feet down the rock face into a shallow, scallop-shaped basin. To the right and left, there were white limestone benches, carved in relief with acanthus leaves.

Helena let out a breath. The simplicity and secrecy of the place were deeply pleasing. She took a step forward to stand alongside Michael's chair, exchanging a smile with him. She thought how well he looked with the afternoon light in his dark eyes and waving hair: mischievous, faun-like amid all the greenery. She had once thought about his always-moving hands as being like flowers pushed by the wind; here in the garden, where everything was in subtle motion, the restless physicality of his limbs seemed natural, vital.

Still wordless, she stepped forward to the fountain and reached out her hands to the slender stream of water, letting it run over her fingers a little while before she brought it to cool her cheeks, her neck. She stood with her back to Michael, feeling his gaze on her.

Once again she rinsed her hands, then cupped one to catch a little water. She turned and approached Michael, and then offered her cupped hand to his lips, automatically reaching to steady the back of his head with her other hand as she did so.

Goosebumps prickled over her skin as she felt the touch of his warm lips through the coolness of the water; he sipped. Slowly she let the fingers of her other hand curl into his hair, grasping it. He had closed his eyes. When he had drunk the water, she slowly turned over her emptied hand, touching the damp fingers to his lips; then she pushed her first two fingers into his mouth. His eyelids trembled, and in response, he pushed his tongue forward to slide against the underside of her fingers. She let out a shaking breath.

The afternoon seemed to have stilled, hushed. She felt as if she were under a magnifying lens. She felt intensely the warmth of his tongue; the crisp hair at the back of his head, through which she traced her other fingers; the touch of the resin-scented air around them.

Having arrived here, she told him, softly: "Tell me what to do." She wanted to be near to him, as near to him as possible; she wanted to be *part* of him, mingling in the same way that shade and sunlight mingled beneath the trees.

He opened his eyes and parted his lips, gently releasing her fingers. His arms were beginning to twist and jerk in his lap, agitated. Without moving his eyes away from hers, he impatiently reached out his left hand until he could grasp the other wrist, containing his movements. "Kiss me," he said. "Please."

She pulled up her dress and knelt in the fine gravel at his feet, then leaned forward to clasp her hands on either side of his face. They kissed for long moments: heated, fierce. His arms shook in between them.

They parted, their breaths blowing warm against each other's faces. Cupping his face, she thought about how this was the first time she had touched him, really, since May—more than two months ago.

As if having the same thought, he said in a low voice, "You've been so far away."

"I'm here," she replied. She didn't let herself feel the full weight of the longing in his words; she wanted to stay in the intensity of touching him, seeing him; she didn't want to think about all the time she might have wasted, all the moments when she could have dared and hadn't.

His eyebrows had drawn together, as if doubting her, and

the sight pained her. She reached to touch his brow, and whispered, "Tell me what you want to do."

His mouth firmed, as if with resolve, and his eyes flickered back over his shoulder before he said, "Help me move to one of the benches."

Silently, she stood back and helped him stand up out of his wheelchair, holding each of his shaking hands firmly. She stepped backwards with him as he took short, jerking steps towards one of the benches, then pivoted effortfully to release his weight downwards, almost collapsing the final distance onto the seat. The urgency of his movements stoked heat within her.

The bench had arms and a back, but Michael had fallen awkwardly into a corner, lolling backwards with his arms half-upraised, so the edges of the white stone must have been pressing into his flesh. Swiftly she bent to help him take off his jacket, folding it behind him for padding.

His eyes were still hot on her; he gestured towards himself with his chin. In response, she climbed to straddle him, inhaling deeply when she felt the heat of his body again. For a little while he fought to control his arms, and she lay still as they writhed around her, his brow furrowed with effort; then he succeeded in recapturing his wrist and pulling his linked arms down around her back, clasping her.

He raised his head towards hers and for long minutes, simply explored her face with his lips, his kisses, tracing his lips over her brow, her eyelids, her cheeks, and every contour of her mouth. She lay against him, desire mounting inside of her, an urgent beat. The long conversations she shared with Michael, the effortless play of words and ideas, they were good, even vital to her—but she needed this with him, too. It was the natural expression of everything that grew between them whenever they shared space, thoughts, glances.

In the heat of the moment, the thought broke into her mind, the thought that she had not allowed herself to admit before: *I can't be just a friend to him.*

And: *As long as I know him, I will desire him.*

She shuddered with desire against him, and she felt an answering groan resonate through his chest.

"Let me see you," he whispered.

She pushed herself up against his chest, so that he had to release his arms, which fell to either side of them. Kneeling above him, she fumbled to undo her dress, but the linen day dress had a high neckline and a row of tiny buttons down the back; she clicked her tongue with impatience and gave up. Instead, she shocked herself by pulling up her skirt, baring her legs— and then, as he was already inhaling sharply, pulled down her stockings and undergarments to truly bare herself to him.

Her cheeks were already heating with discomfiture as she pulled herself up higher above him, but she persisted. His eyes were wide, and he murmured something that she couldn't catch, but the sound of it made her feel as if she were being stroked. She reached down and gently pushed his shoulders until he slid a little further down the armrest, his head pillowed on the jacket. Then she leaned forward, bracing her hands on the armrest, until she could bring her hips close to his face. She felt his breath against her; she felt his body twitching between her legs. Then she felt his tentative kiss, and another, and another. She leaned heavily onto the armrest, the cold stone pressing back into her palms, while she dissolved with pleasure.

There was no particular art to his kissing, no hunt or direction. With simple affection and wonder, he was exploring her, as he had touched her face again and again with his lips.

The gentleness of it—the innocence of it—undid her. She felt as if she were being made anew, there in the heart of the garden.

Somewhere in the haze of pleasure, she whispered his name, and he jerked in reaction, falling back against the bench. "Sorry," she said instantly, chagrined.

He shook his head, looking dazed. "Is something wrong?"

"No, just..." She looked down at his flushed face, his dark glittering eyes, framed between her arms, and yet she couldn't say it.

This time she shook her head, brushed his cheek with one hand, then leaned back and reached to slide both hands down his chest, his belly, coming to rest where he strained against his trousers. She cupped him and watched as he moaned, as his arms flailed in reaction, knocking against the stone of the bench. Chagrined again, she hoped that he hadn't hurt himself—but she went on. She undid his belt, then freed him from his trousers, cupping the hot, velvety flesh.

His eyes had closed, and he seemed to have sunken within himself in reaction to her touch, his body's motions slowing, but when she stroked a thumb against him, he cried out softly with need.

The sound cut her loose. She released him and turned as swiftly as she could—her movements hampered by her lowered stockings—so that she straddled him in the opposite direction, her back to the heat of his chest. She lay back against him, turning her cheek to feel his deep breaths. With one hand she reached until she could find him again, clasping him firmly; with the other hand she reached out until she could find his wandering left hand, and this she brought against herself. "*Yes*," he whispered in her ear.

She nodded mutely, feeling with hot insistence every place where their bodies were connected. And she moved her hand, his hand, stroking both of them closer and closer, as he tensed and jerked under her. "Oh god," she heard him whisper.

He found his climax first; as she felt him begin, she swiftly moved her hand to cover him so that he wouldn't leave telltale stains on their clothing. As she felt his heat surging against her palm, she pushed his left hand a final time against herself, and fell into her own release, panting. Her vision disappeared into a blur of heat, of golden light. She felt him breathing below her, felt his lips press to her neck.

* * *

She came to with a stab of fear: she felt suddenly the fact of their exposure in the garden. She clambered off him unceremoniously, pulling up her stockings, then stumbled briefly on her way to the fountain; she heard his noise of concern behind her. She rinsed off her hands, then returned to help tidy him.

"Sorry," he said softly, as he watched her attend to his wandering hands with her dampened handkerchief.

It was unusual for him to apologize unnecessarily. Was she being too brusque? She looked at him closely, slowing her motions. "What do you mean?"

He smiled thinly. "Just that you have to clean up for the both of us."

She laughed a little, shook her head, and could find nothing to say. She continued with her work.

Her heart was still beating with nervousness, and she could tell this had communicated itself to him; he was glancing about anxiously, as if expecting someone to appear behind her in the entryway in the hedges.

Nonetheless, after she had helped him back into his chair, she couldn't resist bending to embrace him tightly about his shoulders; one of his hands groped up and managed to grasp onto her wrist in response. Her throat felt tight with all the things she wanted to say.

She said nothing; she stood again, pulling away from him slowly, and his hand dropped back down into his lap. She touched it briefly before setting off again. They withdrew from the garden in silence together; the sunlight was turning a darker shade of gold.

* * *

Lying in her bedroom in Delia's house now, Helena thought of Mrs. Byrne quizzing her so eagerly that afternoon about the meaning of the *hortus conclusus*, the enclosed garden. She pressed the heels of her palms to her eyes and groaned aloud. She had heard before of cases of spontaneous combustion; might that be brought on by shame?

Could Mrs. Byrne have sent someone to follow them that day? Surely she couldn't have been so... prurient. Well, it *wouldn't* have been prurient if she and Michael hadn't chosen to do what they had done.

She groaned again. And, like some kind of awful vamp, she hadn't even been able to bring herself to speak to him afterwards...

She shook her head. How much might Mrs. Byrne know? If she had long since guessed the nature of their friendship, she needn't have had them followed—Helena had to banish that mortifying idea. She could simply have guessed what would ensue if Karl were absent. God, and what if she had engineered Karl's absence? No, that was Helena's imagination going a step too far, again. Mrs. Byrne was observant, even calculating, but she was not some sort of decadent, Byzantine schemer, laying a path for Helena to tumble deeper into temptation.

Well, but what about the proposal she had laid before Helena this afternoon? What was that, if not Byzantine in its complexity—and decadent in its implications? A household of four! She knew that Mrs. Byrne was a regular churchgoer; now she wondered if it was all for appearances, or if Mrs. Byrne really did cling to a measure of devoutness—yet had been forced to set aside many of her compunctions in order to shelter her youngest son.

Once again, she shook her head, this time in disbelief at the afternoon's revelations. Did Michael know about Lewis? He must, the two of them were so close; it was clear that Lewis regarded him as a true confidant. Her mind slewed back all of a sudden to Michael's story about his childhood tutor, who had "disgraced himself somehow" at Oxford, but now conducted scholarship with a Frenchman... they were "quite pleased with each other"... Could it be that they were inverts, too? Had Michael also told their story to Lewis, trying to bolster his hopes for his affair with Mr. Plainsborough?

She bit her lip. Speculation, it was all speculation, just her mind lurching about wildly and trying to make sense of the pieces. It wasn't impossible, her speculation about Michael's tutor, but would it make any material difference to her if it were true? Perhaps the trouble was only that she was less worldly than she had thought. She had read her bit of Havelock Ellis during her time in college; a heavy volume of the physician's work on the truth of human sexuality had been passed from hand to hand and subjected to arch recitals among some of the girls who had prided themselves on their status as "new" women. But now, it seemed, she couldn't grapple with the shock that she felt at all these matters being forced into the light before her own eyes.

Perhaps it was only that she wanted to think that her impossible relationship with Michael was somehow singular, untouchable. Now—childishly, selfishly—she felt that it had been spoiled by association with what lay between Lewis Byrne and John Daniel Plainsborough.

Thinking of Lewis' sweet, open face, she beat her palms against her cheeks in recrimination. She must not be so selfish. He must have known unhappiness she couldn't dream of, loving as he did, even if she couldn't yet understand it.

She stilled. From Lewis' situation, her mind had veered to another thought. Helena had been so stunned by Mrs. Byrne's proposal that she had *never asked whether she'd told Lewis or Michael.* Did Lewis know that his mother had proposed to marry him off to his brother's lover? Did Michael know that his mother had proposed to marry his lover off to his brother?

She groaned aloud again. What would happen if she simply bought a train ticket the next morning and departed for Pennsylvania without another word to any of the lot of them? Aunt Delia could arrange for her luggage to be sent after her. She could marry the first New York financier she met off the train and never think about California again.

God, god... was that so stupid a plan, really?

Well, it was stupid if she took stock of the hard knot at the center of things—the knot that even Alexander's sword couldn't have cut through. The knot was this—and now she could see this clearly and truly: she wanted Michael more than any other man she had ever met. And so far, Mrs. Byrne's plan was the only way she could see to spend her life with him, even if meant they would still have to skulk about, even if it meant the servants might always talk, even if it meant an overly sharp-eyed society journalist could open a hellmouth's worth of trouble.

She stared deliriously at the opposite wall, with its wallpaper of birds-of-paradise, its serene Japanese prints floating in black frames.

Several hours later, when there was a gentle knock at the door and Aunt Delia's voice inquired after her, Helena replied thickly that she wouldn't be coming down for dinner. "But don't worry about me, really. My wan Eastern constitution must still be not quite adapted to your Californian sun." She attempted to laugh.

She heard the door open a crack, and squinted through the corner of an eye to see Aunt Delia's head silhouetted in the doorway. She didn't move. The door closed again.

Helena closed her eyes, trying not to imagine that she was resting with her head against Michael's shoulder.

* * *

The following days felt tepid, bruised. Helena found that she did, in fact, often come down with headaches; she sipped water incessantly in an attempt to quell them, or at least symbolically purify herself, and buried herself in work for Aunt Delia's museum. She declined as many social engagements as she could without seeming rude, pleading a desire to make the most of her remaining time with the museum's affairs before she departed.

It was true enough that she would miss the work keenly

when she went back East. In between correspondence, cataloging, and finances, she gazed at the watercolor sketches of exhibits that she had mocked up after the architect's blueprints; Delia had liked them enough that she had had them pinned up on a board for months now. In the imagined vitrines lay Egyptian clay oil lamps and Roman perfume flacons of glass and gold; stemmed Greek wine cups and bronze daggers; seal rings of carnelian and agate; Arab ceramic platters and bowls and vases painted brightly and boldly. There were standing screens of lustrous painted silk paper, heavy doors of wood intricately carved. She found respite by imagining herself wandering, years from now, amid the shining treasures in their curious arrangements, the murmured conversations of patrons echoing from the polished marble floors. It was easy to imagine the cool air, the mellow light, the faint suggestion of incense wafting through the slender-pillared corridors.

But then the questions would arise: how might this future Helena feel; who might be in her thoughts? She could only imagine herself feeling as sour, unsettled, and alone as she felt now. And so, despairingly, she arrived back at her present predicament.

In her diary, she found herself inscribing the number of days before her return train: twelve days, ten, seven... She felt each new numeral like a weight of guilt.

Could she imagine herself as Mrs. Lewis Byrne? Was it so dreadful, so false a thought? Her parents would be pleased, at least: a son of the Byrnes! And he was good-looking, cheerful...

She imagined standing across an altar from Lewis, taking

his arm to be escorted to parties while he smiled his sunny smile, sharing dinnertime conversations linked by a strange complicity: the knowledge that they would each be retiring to a separate bedchamber, a separate companion. Here her mind recoiled: how long could she really tolerate such an arrangement? She wondered how many times Mrs. Byrne herself had traced out tortuous hypotheticals, followed them to any number of possible outcomes, many of them disastrous, or at least humiliating.

But then, there came the thought: how it would feel to go down a quiet, lamp-lighted hallway to find Michael at the end, surrounded by books as always, safe, cherished. How it would feel to know that he was hers, and she was his. To see his smiling face close to hers.

And Lewis would want a house in the city, no doubt, not out in the hills like the Byrne mansion—that would mean that Michael could go out: to the library, museums, gardens, cinemas. Who was to say that together, she and Lewis could not arrange for Michael a more public existence than his parents had so far dared? It would be eccentric, true, for a man to be housing his crippled brother, but perhaps understandable in light of the fact that the Byrnes had no daughters to take on the duties of care. And for every four or five members of high society who would think it most proper for him to live quietly, unseen in the countryside, there might be a broad-minded one who could admit to the benefits of giving him access to city life.

Yet whenever Helena framed these arguments to herself,

she was inevitably left with a sense of shame. Thinking about Michael as if he were a parcel to be passed from hand to hand; having to defend to an imagined interlocutor the idea that he, like any other man, might want to be able to leave his house and enjoy the amusements of a city... it was all depressing, degrading.

And so her thoughts would make the final turn: to the image of flight. She might depart California without another word to any of the Byrnes; she could spend the autumn and winter in Philadelphia, alone and unburdened.

Unburdened! There was a joke. How could she ever be unburdened when she knew that back in California, there was Michael, more alone than she would ever be?

And so the wheel began turning again. As if in a cage, Helena paced around and around, circling the axis of her misery.

* * *

Three days before her departure, Helena asked Aunt Delia to take her one last time to the museum site, to fix its image in her mind. It would be much changed before she saw it again, in half a year or more.

It was late August. The two women stood on the hillside under the shade of the oaks where Helena had once seen the workmen take their lunch. The site was deserted for the weekend, and so it took on more than ever the quality of a newly discovered ruin. Ladders and coils of rope lay about.

The foundations now stood several feet above the ground, and stacks of pine planks awaited use as scaffolding or ramps.

Helena gazed about slowly. The pure California sunlight already bore a nostalgic quality for her, as if she were looking at a memory from a year ago. Soon, instead, she would see autumn downpours and fogs, winter sleet. But here, the foundations of Aunt Delia's museum lay shining white-gold under the expanse of the sky.

Suddenly she found that tears were sliding down her cheeks. She put a hand to her mouth, and tried to be quiet.

In another moment, she felt Aunt Delia's arm around her shoulder. The taller woman drew her close, and Helena instinctually turned her to press her face against her breast, so that she could hide her face and cry.

"My dear Helena," Aunt Delia said after a little time, "won't you tell me what's the matter?"

Helena's defenses were gone. She pulled back her face enough to say, "I was looking around the museum and think-ing... there will be so many stairs. Michael will never be able to visit."

"Oh, my dear," said Aunt Delia.

The tone of her voice made Helena start crying again. "Sorry... I'm sorry."

"Please don't apologize. You've loved him for a long time, haven't you?" Aunt Delia held her shoulders warmly.

"From the first night I met him." Saying the words brought a fresh spate of tears, but also a deep sense of relief, of disburdening. She clasped her aunt tightly, feeling gratitude well up within her.

When Helena pulled back, trying to compose herself, she found that Aunt Delia had was offering her a handkerchief, and she took it gratefully. "The first night..." she found herself repeating. It was as if she needed to test out the words again. It was, after all, her first time really speaking of her feelings: Mrs. Byrne had not been interested in declarations of love.

Aunt Delia watched her; her heavy-lidded grey eyes were solemn. "I can see that. He's a remarkable man. He lives with principles and vigor, despite all his constraints. And it's clear that you make each other very happy. But now—what has made you so sad? Is it—very reasonably—the thought of leaving him? Or did Catherine say something to you?"

"Oh, you've guessed it," Helena said, trying to laugh. "I'd be a terrible spy." She wiped her eyes again and blew out a long, shaky breath, trying to rid herself of the excess of emotion.

She continued, "It was Mrs. Byrne. She... she asked me if I would consider marrying Lewis... so that I could still be... close to Michael if I chose."

Aunt Delia's brows came together. "Marrying *Lewis*. I *see*. And how did that make you feel?"

"Oh, god. Like I had too many choices, and yet no choices at all."

"Yes, I can see that. And so—what is it you think you want, now? Other than fewer steps in the museum."

This time, Helena laughed a real laugh. "Thank you. Oh...

what do I want. I want to run away. But I also want to be with Michael."

Aunt Delia paused, considering. "And what have you said to Michael about all this?"

"Nothing," Helena whispered miserably. She wanted to crawl inside of herself. "I don't even know if his mother said anything to him about her proposal. Him, or Lewis."

Aunt Delia shook her head, frowning slightly. She was tapping the long fingers of one hand against the palm of the other. "Yes, it's doubly complicated now—or triply. And I can certainly see why you would have hesitated to say anything to Michael, even before Catherine's proposal."

"I... what could I imagine offering him? I couldn't promise him anything. My parents..." Into her mind came the image that she had often had to suppress: how her parents would react the first time they saw Michael's trembling, writhing body.

Delia looked at her consideringly. "You're not as close with your mother as you used to be, are you?"

Helena shifted, uncomfortable. "You're right. Ever since I broke off that engagement... She said things then that I've found... difficult to forgive."

"I'd guessed it was something like that. You've barely mentioned her all summer. Oh, I'm sorry, Helena, I don't mean to keep sticking pins into you when you've already come to me belly-up. I'm just trying to put together all the pieces in my mind... It's not an uncomplicated situation you've found yourself in." They shared a rueful laugh.

Aunt Delia gestured that she was going to take a seat

on the rocks, and Helena followed her lead. She gripped her hands together tightly in her lap. "So where does this all leave us," Aunt Delia resumed. "Your parents are looking for you to make an advantageous match. They also feel that you—sorry, my dear—have disappointed them once before. Does that now mean that the margin for error, with a second try, is smaller? Or greater?"

"You mean, have they given up on me making sensible choices? Yes and no at the same time, I think. They dread me bringing more trouble for them... but they also expect it."

Aunt Delia gave her a wry look. "You'll know I speak from experience when I say that I know what you mean."

Helena smiled in answer.

"Well, well... If you couldn't tell from my scattershot inquisition, my thoughts are all in disarray," Aunt Delia went on. "I can't imagine that yours could be any different... and so I will attempt to simplify."

"I feel as if I'm awaiting an oracle," Helena remarked, widening her eyes with anticipation, not really exaggerated.

Aunt Delia mimed wafting visionary fumes towards herself. "Well, here it comes. But I can't promise Delphic quality.

"First, and practically speaking: *if* you decide that what you really want for yourself, lies with the Byrne family—remember that Mrs. Byrne would levy every resource at her disposal to ensure the well-being of any of her sons. I realize you're not fond of her queenly airs, but she is, in her own way, an unorthodox woman. She's had difficult decisions to make with her sons, and with little interest or care from her husband. I can't claim that I know what I would have done, in her situation. But I think that she loves all of her sons so deeply that it hurts her, and it makes her afraid to show it."

Helena nodded slowly, touched and a little chastened.

"Second," Aunt Delia continued, "I think you already know what you really want. And maybe that's what I should have said first."

Helena kissed her aunt's cheek. "No, it's perfect: this way it will keep ringing in my head. Thank you, Aunt Delia."

"Oh, but one more thing: *whatever* you decide, you must know that I will support you. I am perhaps not the most scrupulous of chaperones, but I am nonetheless devoted to your interests."

"I would never, ever doubt it. Oh, Aunt Delia, how can I deserve you?" Helena reached out for her aunt's hands. "I wish..."

"Wish what?" Aunt Delia regarded her fondly.

Helena had been thinking of a shy, serious Moorish boy standing in a bustling medina, gazing through shafting sunlight at the figure of her young aunt, clad in girlish white... but then she looked at her aunt now: serene, always brimming with a secret joy, alone yet never lonely.

She said, "Oh, never mind. But I do love you."

"You know very well what my response is, my dear." Aunt Delia smiled and rose to her feet, still holding one of Helena's hands; with the other, she shook out her skirt. Helena followed suit.

As they prepared to go, Aunt Delia seemed to look about

the museum site with a newly critical gaze. "I *do* wish you had mentioned something earlier about all the steps. I simply wasn't thinking."

"I was afraid. Now I know I was silly to think you might think I was being unreasonable." Helena clasped her aunt's hand tightly one more time, then gently released it.

"Well, it's not too late to make a change... I am optimistic that Miss Montague will find it an interesting challenge, and hardly an obstacle."

The two women began picking their way back down the hillside to the car. A scrub jay called; the museum lay behind them, raw and shining, ready to make something new of the past.

* * *

Helena telephoned Byrne mansion the next morning. Through the hiss and ghostly chatter of the phone line, she told Mrs. Byrne simply, "I'd like to speak to Michael. Today."

"I see," Mrs. Byrne said with admirably little hesitation. "Please do come by." In the sea of hissing, it was impossible to read her tone.

A little over an hour later, Helena strode into Michael's gallery—but she regretted her swiftness as she registered the startling sight of him standing up at one of his bookshelves.

One of his hands was gripped around the edge of a shelf for balance, but as soon as he saw her, he jerked backwards violently, losing his hold; that arm curled in towards his chest. At the same time, one of his always-bent knees buckled further, and he began to fall towards the shelves, letting out a wordless exclamation.

Helena and Karl, who had been standing in the opposite doorway, each rushed forward and reached him at about the same time. Michael's shoulder and head had already struck the shelf, though not with great force, and then Karl was there, gripping him under the arms and swiftly pulling him back to rest him in his wheelchair.

Karl raised his eyes to Helena, and, for the first time, gave her a look of disapproval, even disappointment.

Helena was flushed with distress, but forced herself to meet Karl's look squarely, acknowledging it, before turning to Michael. "I'm *so* sorry. I didn't think. Please accept my apology. Are you hurt?"

He was lying awkwardly in his wheelchair, his limbs jerking as the shock of her sudden appearance continued to work its way through him, but he gave her a wry look. "Mostly my pride, but I think you know that's rather resilient."

Helena didn't laugh. "I really am awfully sorry. Both of you." She knew that he was accustomed to frequent bruises and scrapes, but she abhorred her carelessness, on today of all days in particular.

Michael shook his head, signaling resignation, at the same time that Karl nodded slightly.

Michael had collected himself enough to be able to draw his feet together, pushing himself up to sit straighter in his chair.

"Well, and what brings you upon us so precipitately? Are the Persians invading Greece again?"

Helena couldn't resist a smile. "No, we don't have any need of aid from Sparta—yet. But I do need to speak with you." She steeled herself and, for the first time that year, said, "Karl—would you mind leaving us, please?"

Karl's and Michael's eyebrows had both gone up, and they exchanged a look before Karl said quietly, "Of course, Miss De Vries." He inclined his head and withdrew towards the rest of the house. Once again, Helena wondered how much Michael ever divulged to Karl.

Left alone in the gallery, Helena and Michael faced each other. He was looking at her inquiringly. One of his arms lay in his lap, while the other was thrust out to one side, jerking. Helena had clasped her own hands together uncertainly. "Could we go into the conservatory? I would like it if we were somewhere that felt a bit less—exposed." In the high-ceilinged gallery, she felt as if every sound echoed.

Michael raised his eyebrows again, but said, "Of course." She waited while he turned himself about, pushing the wheelchair with one foot, then set off pulling himself towards the little fern-filled conservatory on the other side of the gallery. They proceeded in silence except for the occasional creak from his chair.

"You're leaving us in two days," was all he said once she'd seated herself. He leaned back in his chair.

She drew in a breath. "Yes." His tone was so neutral, even light, as if he expected nothing, and had nothing to show.

"So, is this 'good-bye,' or even 'good-bye for now'?"

"I... no, it's more than that." He was beginning to look wary. "I wanted to ask you some questions."

He nodded for her to continue. His arms twisted at his sides.

"Michael... Did your mother say anything to you? About *us*?"

His brows had drawn together. "No," he said, "nothing out of the ordinary. What is it? What did she say to you?" His arms had begun moving faster.

She licked her lips; her heart was beating painfully. "She... Michael, she asked me if I would marry Lewis."

He spasmed with shock, his dark eyes rolling back as his back arched and his arms flung themselves outward, jerking frantically. She heard his breath go hoarse, and a groan came from his chest. The sound cut her.

She leaned forward and touched her hands to his knees, willing her body to lend him warmth—except that she was afraid her hands were icy with nervousness. "Michael." His eyes met hers, bewildered. "Michael, she asked me if I would do it... because she wants to protect Lewis, because of his... inclination, but also so that I could be as close to *you* as I wanted. She... she said it because she knew about us, and she wanted to offer a way for us to be close together."

She waited, distraught, while he fought to control his body again. She listened to his laboring breath, the rustling of his body.

When he was finally able to regain a measure of physical

composure, he said, "Well, I should have known it wouldn't get by Mother."

She choked out a laugh. "I thought the same thing." She leaned forward and carefully captured one of his hands, pressing it between both of hers; he gave her a grateful look, and she had to keep herself from falling into the simple comfort of it. She pushed onward: "But—what else do you think?"

He shook his head disbelievingly. "I don't even know if I could say. It's—well. I'm a little overwhelmed."

"Well, before you've attempted to grapple with the particulars, it might be most expedient if I just whelm you again. Michael—*I don't want to do it.* But maybe not for the reason that you think. It's not that I'm afraid of... of tying myself to you in any fashion...

She tried to lay out her thoughts clearly. "Lewis—I know Lewis has his own predicament to face. But it's not mine. Michael, I don't want Lewis, I want you. I love you, and I want to marry you or no one at all."

The words came out in a rush, and she hated that her voice sounded trembling and childish to her own ears, when she wanted him to feel the certainty that she felt at her core, the certainty that Aunt Delia had seen.

She held his hand tightly as he struggled on the crest of another wave of spasms. Again and again his eyes came back to hers, disbelieving, and her heart twisted when she saw that he was fighting back tears.

"God!" he exclaimed when he had somewhat recovered. "To be able to have a conversation, *uninterrupted...*"

She brought his hand to her lips and kissed it in answer.

"Helena," he said, his voice low and urgent. "Helena, Helena. I love you. I do love you, with all of me. I hope that when I die, I will do so remembering the moment that you told me that you love me. But—it would never work. It can't work."

"Why not?" she said, trying to sound unconcerned.

"Because... this is the best way for me to live." And he indicated the room around them with his chin.

When she saw his gaze lingering on the cage of softly chattering finches in the corner, she said teasingly, "The metaphor's a bit on the nose, don't you think?"

"Oh, stop. Nobody invited you here for literary criticism."

"I thought you said you loved me with all of yourself." Even as she teased him, she felt the words fill her with a rush of emotion again.

"I didn't specify that I loved all of *you*. Oh, we have to stop this nonsense."

"We do. Michael, think of it. What if we didn't have to sneak around? What if we could go out together? What if *you* could go out, simply?"

Michael smiled uncertainly. "I... I don't know if I even want that. Helena, it's been so long. We talked about this even the first night that we met: I'm accustomed to the shape of my life. It's easy for you to say, 'Michael ought to go out more'... but, god. The way people would *stare*... Hardly anybody has ever met someone who looks like me. Even plenty of doctors haven't."

He shook his head laboriously, then continued, "It's easy for me to joke about having no pride when I'm safe here, where everybody knows me. But I *do* have my pride. And I know you do, too. Imagine trying to go out, to... to a restaurant, a shop, somewhere ordinary, filled with all sorts of people. Imagine expecting them not to stare, not to sneer or be disgusted or horrified. And forget about strangers—what would your *parents* think? Imagine the first time they find out you think you want to marry a man who can't even feed himself his own dinner. Could I tolerate it? Could *you?*"

He was looking at her piercingly.

Helena had steeled herself not to flinch at those words, at the images that had filled her mind time and time again. His sinewy hand twitched urgently within her grasp. "I don't know. It's true I don't know, Michael. But... we haven't even had a chance to try. I don't mean to be... Joan of Arc or something, throwing myself on a pyre for the sake of an ideal, a voice in my head. I just want a chance for us to try to live like an ordinary man and an ordinary woman who... who are in love with each other. I look at you, and I think about you, and I think to myself... what a *waste*. What a waste for someone so sharp and curious, and so feeling, and so handsome—don't make that face—to be tucked away in the back corner of a house as if there weren't more he could do in the world. Your mother won't even admit that you understand the family business, but I've seen your conversations with Lewis about it. He's clever, but he can't take the long view, he can only make decisions for next Tuesday or next month. If it were only Lewis in the game, your family would only have a tactician, but because he comes to you so much for help, you've made him look like a strategist. Somebody ought to acknowledge that."

Michael looked almost angry, his face flushed, sweat standing out on his brow, his free hand beating itself against his own chest. Helena slowed the flood of her words, chagrined, and yet her certainty ran through her like a thread of fire. "I'm sorry! I'm sorry. I don't mean to lecture you on your own family, or slight your brother. I just... when I think about you, the truth of you, I don't understand why the way your body is—should be treated as if it made *any* material difference. Especially not—oh, this is vulgar, but I'll just say it—especially not when your family is as famously rich as they are. Money has made the difference in plenty of other curious cases. Why not *here*?"

Michael let out a long breath, leaning back into his chair. In the corner, the finches made inquisitive chirring sounds, alarmed by the raised voices in their sanctuary. "You've been thinking about this," Michael observed, "for a long time."

"How could I not?"

"Helena, you must understand that all of this comes as a little shock, considering that I couldn't tell the seriousness of your feelings for me all summer, and in fact, being with me sometimes seemed to make you sadder than when you first came. And please understand that I don't mean this as a complaint. It would have been strange for a young woman of your station *not* to be a little guarded in a situation like... this."

"I... I don't think I meant to be guarded. I thought I was sharing myself with you. I *meant* to. I'm only realizing now that

I couldn't, because all along I wanted to say all of *this*. Only I didn't realize everything I was thinking... And even if I had, I would have been afraid to say it. I got blocked up."

Michael was shaking his head slowly again, bewildered. "Helena, I feel as if someone's spun my head around three times, at least. Where are we supposed to go from here?"

For an answer, she kissed him. He responded, melting into her, his clenched arm relaxing downward. They kissed again and again, deeply and slowly.

Michael was the first to draw away, but he did so with visible reluctance. "Well," he said softly, "you make an excellent argument."

She looked down, gently stroking her fingertips over the back of his hand. Then she lifted his hand to fit it around her cheek, welcoming the intermittent pressure as his fingers flexed against her. "Michael, I'm not saying that we should march into your mother's study and demand a society wedding next Tuesday. I just... would it really be so much to ask for something like a normal courtship?" He rearranged himself in his chair, looking tense and uncomfortable, and she hastened to add encouragement: "I already know that Aunt Delia would support us—with both your mother and my parents. It wouldn't be us, alone..."

He was silent; he seemed to be turning something over in his mind. She rested his hand in her lap and watched him, suppressing the urge to chatter nervously. Once, his head dropped forward to loll across his chest, but he seemed to ignore it.

Eventually he looked up. His hand pulled away from hers,

whether voluntarily or not she couldn't tell. "Helena, will you tell me one thing? Last year... what happened to your engagement?"

She tensed; a jolt of anxiety went through her chest. "I would have thought you'd have heard all the gossip already," she said bitterly, thinking of his conversations with the servants.

He moved impatiently, his arms splaying apart. "I'd rather hear it from you."

She put a hand to her neck and looked to one side, thinking. Her cheeks were hot with shame, and her mouth was compressed.

Finally she began, "His name was Paul, but maybe you already knew that. We met when I was still in finishing school; he was two years older than me, already in college. He saw me at a dance when he was visiting back for his sister's engagement. For the rest of his visit, he followed me around as much as he could. Once he started writing me letters, I started liking the attention—they could be quite beautiful. I don't think he copied them from books or his friends the way some boys did; he had original ways of putting things, funny little turns of phrase. And he told me I made him feel like he could share things he'd never shared before.

"We both went to college in New York. My parents were excited about him from early on, as soon as I hinted that he was paying me any attention; he was from just the right kind of family, *et cetera*.

"I loved being in New York, and I especially liked being in New York with him—it made me feel sophisticated, womanly, all those tawdry words. It made me feel like I knew where my life was going, and it was going to be clean and dazzling. I could picture where we would be in ten years.

"We got engaged. He had a car; we went out often together."

She was still looking away from Michael, staring at the patterns in the black-and-white tiled floor, at the soft, dense shadows of the foliage cast over it.

"When I reached my junior year, and he'd graduated, something changed. I could feel him watching me all the time; I could tell he was annoyed, but I didn't know why. He started making all these little remarks, little jabs and cuts. He would tell me that... I didn't really care about what I was studying, I just liked to be able to tell people lots of 'facts,' that I liked being able to hold things over people's heads." She said *facts* the way he had, with a derisive drawl, drawing out the *f* and the *s*. "Or he would start by asking me lots of questions about something I was excited about, and then stop halfway through and give me this little smile to tell me that he hadn't cared at all about anything I had said, he'd just wanted to wind me up.

"I didn't know what to do. He'd always been encouraging to me before." She paused, running her fingernails edgewise up and down the side of her neck, liking the distraction of the slight pain.

"Eventually it came out in a fight... He didn't like that I was serious about finishing college. He'd thought it was cute that I wanted to go at all, he liked being able to brag about me being pretty *and* brainy, but, you know, I was drifting into the vicinity of the girl who's *too* brainy. The men at his office made jokes about it. He wanted me to drop out, marry him, have done.

"I thought about it for a while. What did I think I was really going to do with a degree in history, anyway?

"But I went for a walk by myself one afternoon in Central Park and realized… I'd felt cold and sad for months. I'd been too ashamed to try to explain it to any of my friends. I felt like I didn't even know how to talk to anyone anymore because no matter what I said, if Paul was there, he'd find a way to turn it into a dig at me. I just wanted him to hold me and be quiet because it was the only time I didn't feel attacked. And that afternoon I realized, I never wanted him to hold me again, either.

"So that was that." She shrugged. "I'm not sure if you expected to hear something else." She finally looked back up at him, and the look on his face was so heavy that she felt compelled to add, "So now I have a history degree and no husband. Unless you'd like to do something about that."

He didn't smile. He reached out his left hand for hers; as it wavered back and forth, she intercepted it, and his fingers grasped hers spasmodically. "I'm sorry, Helena. He was cruel to you. I'm only glad you ended it, even if it cost you dearly to do it."

She brought his hand to her lips and kissed its back in silent thanks. Then she couldn't resist probing again: "Was that what you expected to hear?"

A grimace crossed briefly over his face, and he averted his eyes, his head listing over to one shoulder. "I admit," he said slowly, "I had wondered if he had done something like... like striking you in anger, or chasing another woman. Something that..." His eyes met hers again for a moment, before dropping again—in shame, she thought.

Something that you would never be able to do, Helena thought, after a few seconds' reflection. He looked up, and clearly saw that she understood his implication.

As if to demonstrate, his body spasmed then, his legs thrusting his hips out of the seat, his hand tugging away from hers without quite escaping her grasp, his other arm casting out wildly, jerking in and out, before thumping down against the side of his chair. As he settled again, he pushed out a hard breath through his nose and met her gaze, his mouth pressed into a line. "Yes," he said, as if she'd spoken aloud. "You'll forgive me if I say... one can't help but continue to question why you would be attracted to me."

She sighed and leaned forward to wrap her arms around his shoulders. She felt very tired all of a sudden. She rested her forehead against his neck, grateful to feel his warmth seep up into her. "Michael, my dear Michael. Don't ask me to explain it. I only know that I know what it feels like to be desperately unhappy with someone who is supposed to love you; and I know that I feel the deepest happiness when I hear your voice, when I see you, when I am with you."

She heard his breath catch, felt his chest shake; she felt him turn his head and press his lips to her hair. "Helena," was all he said.

"The summer," she said after a little time, "is almost over.

We should go speak to your mother. We should see what can be done."

"Yes," he said, "we should."

Once more, they kissed. Then she disentangled herself from him and stood, watching the finches flutter and cock their heads in the corner, as Michael straightened himself in his chair, pulled himself back into the gallery with his feet. She heard him call out for Karl. After another minute, she heard them conferring quietly; the sound of their voices faded as she sank deeper into herself. She could feel that she was on the brink of a happiness that was as great as it was fragile.

When she heard Michael calling her name from some distance away, she blinked and shook herself. She hastened through the sunlit gallery as she realized that Karl had already helped move both Michael and his wheelchair down the short flight of stairs at its opposite end. On the landing halfway down the steps, she paused and touched one hand to the carved wood paneling, as if to confirm its reality; she felt her heels sinking into the deep green foliate carpeting. Here, three months ago, she had first seen Michael Byrne sitting, watching her in the darkness; now she saw his face, sunlit, at the bottom of the stairs, his eyes fixed on her with a fierce hope.

* * *

"I can't do it. I can't. I can't." Michael struggled in her arms, his eyes staring with panic, his body moving so wildly that she could hardly keep hold of him. Again and again Helena strained to wrap her arms around his chest or his neck, to press him to her breast, as if she could absorb the furious energy that animated his body and made him writhe against his bed, panting, every limb contorted.

In less than an hour, Helena's mother was to arrive for dinner with the Byrnes. She was to meet Michael for the first time: Michael, who was now so panic-stricken by the prospect that he looked like an animal struggling in a trap. *But the trap is his own body,* Helena thought with a fresh stab of emotion.

Mrs. De Vries had arrived that morning after four days of travel by train across the States. She had planned a scant few hours of rest at her hotel to freshen herself before departing the city for the Byrne mansion. Helena typically appreciated her mother's sense of efficiency, but in this case, the rapidity with which she had swept clear her social calendar and arranged her departure for the West Coast had been disquieting. It bespoke the urgency with which she felt she needed to appraise her daughter's would-be betrothed.

Just over two weeks ago, Helena had sent home a long letter in which she announced her desire to become engaged to one of the scions of one of America's foremost families—and described the nature of that particular scion. The balance of frankness and delicacy with which she had endeavored to write about Michael had been the work of hours of deliberation with both him and Aunt Delia. Michael, meanwhile, had himself labored for hours to compose a letter expressing his own hopes, and making every attempt to demonstrate the qualities of character that Helena fiercely reminded him out-weighed whatever might be thought of his physical person.

And now Helena's mother was to descend upon them with what felt like whirlwind speed, to examine Michael in every particular.

Three hours ago, Helena understood, Michael had presented every appearance of composure, even a measured excitement, for the evening ahead.

Two hours earlier, Mrs. Byrne had rung Delia's residence to ask for Helena. "He needs you," was all she had said when Helena took the earpiece.

"I understand," Helena had said evenly, but her heart had filled with dread.

She had rung her mother with the flimsiest of excuses for her early departure to the Byrne mansion. It helped that she had not yet actually gone to meet her mother at the hotel, and so did not have to excuse herself in person. (Her mother had pointedly chosen to stay at a hotel, declining to lodge with Delia, and Helena feared this was a rebuke to her aunt. If Delia had been a more scrupulous chaperone to her niece, surely Helena would never have entertained a courtship with a person bearing "physical defects of a striking magnitude," as one of Mrs. De Vries' letters had had it.)

Upon Helena's arrival at the Byrne mansion, Mrs. Byrne—white-faced and wordless—had conducted her back to Michael's room, where he lay trembling in bed, with Karl hovering beside him.

Everyone had hoped that Helena's arrival would help to

calm Michael. But when he had seen her, his dark eyes flashing white around the rims, it was as if the reality of the situation had broken in upon him afresh, and he lost any remaining control of his nerves. He had let out a terrible moan, his body breaking into a storm of motion.

"Leave me," he had gasped. "Leave me alone."

Helena had met the eyes of Mrs. Byrne and Karl in turn. Without saying anything, the two others had departed the room.

Helena had remained. As she had clambered into the bed with Michael, a sliver of her mind had been grateful that she had worn a gown of heavy satin; it would not betray her exertions by wrinkling or tearing.

"Michael, Michael, I'm here," she had whispered, blinking back tears, trying to keep her voice from trembling.

She had been trying now for over a quarter of an hour to hold him as he writhed against her. Exhausted and torn with sorrow, she thought again how like a wild animal his body was. Her throat ached from trying to hold back tears and from whispering to him, speaking to him, humming, anything that she thought might help.

"I can't do it," Michael repeated hoarsely, his eyes staring at nothing. But as his voice threaded away, she thought that this time, his breathing might be slowing, that his limbs might finally be softening...

She was out of ideas. All she could do now was keep holding him, and breathe, forcing each inhalation, each exhalation to be slow, deliberate, deep. She shut her eyes and felt his feverish warmth. She listened as his own breath slowed and slowed, until it finally matched hers, and he lay lax in her arms.

She heard his ragged voice again. "Can I please have some water?"

She let out a long, shuddering breath of relief. "Of course." She kept one arm lying about his neck and reached out the other to pour him a glass from the carafe by his bed. She propped his head to help him sip from the straw. He closed his eyes as he drank, but when he opened them again, they slid to meet hers, and he searched her face for a long while.

He murmured, "I'm so glad you're here. When you first arrived, I confess I wasn't sure if you were really here."

Helena gave a small smile. "You didn't seem entirely pleased to see me then."

He grimaced. "I wasn't... myself. It's been a difficult few hours."

"That's putting it mildly." She kissed his face. "I'm so sorry, Michael. Do you... do you still feel you can go on with tonight? It's too late to tell my mother not to come here, but I can intercept her, put her off dinner somehow. Or tell her that dinner's to be with your mother alone. I'm sure I can do it without raising a fuss." She wasn't at all sure. "Maybe it's too soon. I understand if... if this all feels like too much to you, and I've pushed things too far..."

"It's too late to turn back, Helena. God, is this what being a real person feels like?"

She frowned. "What do you mean?"

"Didn't you tell me something like that the first night we

met? You said that you had a fear that you had never been a real person, or wouldn't become a real person."

"Oh." She pressed her lips together; it sounded so childish now. "I had hoped you'd forgotten that."

"I didn't. It struck me very much at the time. By 'reality,' I took you to mean something like authenticity—you wanted to be someone like your aunt, you said, who is so very much herself. Or Thoreau—'to live deep and suck out all the marrow of life'..."

Helena nodded. She was simultaneously touched and bewildered. Why was Michael philosophizing now, of all times? Then it occurred to her that he might be pursuing thought as a sort of calming ritual, a way to come back to himself, as he lay limp in her arms.

"And I thought, how curious that this clever and lovely person, who has lived in the world, feels that she lacks reality. What a tricky test reality is, with so many tints and degrees of attainment.

"You see—*I* have never felt myself to be real, because I have never once had the opportunity to make a decision of any consequence. Oh, I'm lucky enough to be able to choose what I want to eat for dinner, or what I want to wear tomorrow. But I've never been able to make a decision that changed *anything* about my life that was in the least serious."

He was speaking quickly now, his low voice growing fierce and urgent.

"You, Helena, presented me with my first opportunity to

make a real decision: would I like to try to follow you into the world, or not?

"To that, I see now that that I must choose to say *yes* not once, but again and again. I must say *yes* even when my body says *no*. So I say to you tonight, Helena: yes, I will have dinner with your mother, and yes, I will do everything in my power to convince her that she wouldn't be thoroughly mad to allow you to marry me.

"And besides." His tone had lightened. "When you came to-night—I told you to leave, but you stayed. You stayed with me. I think it's only fair that I return the favor now, don't you?"

"Oh, Michael." Helena held him tighter. A sob was rising in her chest, and she shook a little as she suppressed it. She bent her head to kiss him. "Yes. We'll do it, then."

After a minute of quiet, Helena helped Michael sit upright. She cooled his face and neck with a damp cloth.

She eyed the clock with concern: just under half an hour till her mother's arrival. "We ought to call Karl to help you dress for dinner, don't you think?" He was still wearing a linen day suit, now rumpled and sweat-damp.

"We should," he said with a sigh. She could see him sum-moning effort, until he slowly lifted his left hand to touch her cheek; she caught it and pressed it there before it could drop back down again. "Will you reassure my mother that I'm fit to go on?"

"I will."

"And then—" Michael made a show of rolling his head on his neck, as if he were getting ready for a fight, even as his hands lay limp, palm-up, in his lap, "—the curtain will rise on *your* mother. Such an awful lot of mothers we have to wrangle."

Helena made a face. "We should be glad our fathers have chosen to wash their hands of the matter, so far," she said ominously.

"Well, paternal silence has been hard-won in these parts. I meant to tell you: the servants tell me Mother launched *another* tremendous quarrel with Father last night about including me in the business. I'm given to understand the pans in the kitchen were just about rattling—and there hasn't been a peep from him since. I'm not sure if he pitched a tent somewhere on the grounds to get away from her. I'm sorry, I'm nattering. Please do go give the cue to Karl and Mother." And then he added, "I love you."

The words still had a forbidden savor. She stroked his cheek. "I love you. Good luck."

Reluctantly, she withdrew her hand and hurried from the room.

* * *

As the remains of the salmon tartare were removed, and the duck à l'orange and two bottles of Côte du Rhone brought in, Helena sensed that the ground had been ceded to her mother.

An exquisite menu had been prepared, and both Helena and Mrs. Byrne had readied a variety of the sort of artfully in-offensive remarks that could nudge a foundering conversation back into safer waters. But there was no way to deflect the central thrust of the dinner, which was Mrs. De Vries' exacting appraisal of Michael Byrne. It was no longer the time for mildly witty exchanges about Mrs. De Vries' travel, the weather in Philadelphia, recent construction in Los Angeles, and so on. Michael had acquitted himself charmingly, of course. (Helena was breathless with a mixture of anxiety and pride.)

Mrs. De Vries had satisfied herself that the crippled Byrne son could, at a minimum, conduct a reasonable conversation. Her questions increasingly focused on Michael, and became more and more pointed. She was taking control of the conversation—and had to be allowed to do so in order for the evening to reach any conclusion.

Mrs. Agnes De Vries was seated opposite Michael. She wore black silk and garnets. She and Helena looked much alike, pale with brown eyes and dark hair (Mrs. De Vries' now bearing several streaks of silver), but Mrs. De Vries was taller and more sharply built than Helena. She had a long neck; the way she inclined her head now to watch Michael made her look faintly predatory, like a heron eyeing a fish about to dart within reach.

When Helena was younger, she had often thought how fortunate she was that her sharp, playful, inquisitive mother could feel more like a sister than a parent. But after Helena had broken her engagement, her mother's humor could turn caustic, and her interest in her daughter's life had begun to feel oppressive. Helena had distanced herself. She hadn't realized how flattened this had made her feel until she had come to California. Even then, she hadn't begun to emerge from her wary torpor... until she had met Michael.

She watched him now, anxious, while she cut her duck into smaller and smaller slivers and occasionally forced herself to swallow a bite.

Michael looked exhausted, his eyes heavy and face pale, his body still eerily limp in his wheelchair. In the days preceding the dinner, they had discussed whether he ought to have Karl strap him in the look of the broad leather straps still made Helena uncomfortable, even if they made Michael feel more composed. But the debate had proved irrelevant: now, the only movements were an occasional stirring from his legs and the curling of the fingers of his right hand, once more cuffed at the wrist by his other hand.

When he was this exhausted, Helena reflected that Michael's movements were less strange, less likely to alarm those unused to him—but he looked *ill*, worn-out and fragile. Only his gaze conveyed the vitality that normally ran through him.

Every now and then, Michael glanced back over his shoulder at Karl, who would step forward and fluidly, soundlessly cut a mouthful and lift it to his master's lips. Michael would chew, and transfer his attention back to the conversation; Karl stepped back to wait again.

Mrs. De Vries was too terrifyingly well-bred to register more than usual interest in any of these proceedings, but still she watched everything, her eyes glinting.

For the past several minutes, she had been inquiring about the family corporation. Her questions were light and typically ended in admiration of the family's success, but nonetheless obliged Michael to demonstrate his understanding of the business' scope, strategy, and aspirations.

Finally she said, "And what, may I ask, is your role or specialty in the business?" Helena detected a suggestion of consolation in her mother's voice, as if she were already preparing to express understanding if Michael replied that he did not, in fact, work. Helena thought this richly unfair, considering how many young men of their social standing never even bothered to pretend that they were interested in working.

Michael shifted in his chair; Helena could tell he was trying to hold his shoulders and head more upright, but he was still listing to one side. He said carefully, "Until recently, I worked for my father simply in an informal advisory capacity—supporting my younger brother's management of the Los Angeles office. We are... solidifying plans to make that position more formal."

"How exciting," said Mrs. DeVries. "I congratulate you, and trust everything will proceed smoothly. And so, does that mean you'll be traveling more often to Los Angeles for business?" Helena suppressed a wince at "more often." She was unsure if Michael had been to Los Angeles even half a dozen times in his lifetime. "Or even taking up residence there? As beautiful as your family estate is, I imagine that the city might hold distinct interest for a young man like yourself." It was impossible to detect whether she placed any unusual emphasis on the phrase "like yourself."

Michael gave a bland smile. "There are many possibilities

for advancing my involvement, and we shall be discussing them. I'm afraid it's too soon yet for me to say more with any certainty."

"Helena has always preferred to live in a city, it's seemed to me, and the bigger, the better," Mrs. De Vries remarked. "We thought we might never recover her from New York. Imagine our surprise when she decamped for the West Coast. But then, she's always been terribly fond of my brother's sister."

"It's difficult not to be," Michael said. "Miss Delia is beyond charming, and wonderfully well-traveled."

"But come, you mustn't praise others at the expense of discussing your own good news," Mrs. De Vries chided. "With this new business responsibility, will your fall be excessively busy? Will you have to re-think a great many social engagements? I can imagine you will want plenty of time to focus. My husband becomes a veritable hermit when he has a new project at hand, and it's only through the greatest of efforts that I can remind him that society will offer refreshment."

"I confess that my calendar," Michael said, "has never been overburdened with social engagements to begin with." This time, in his smile there was a hint of the wryness that Helena liked so much; she couldn't decide how her mother might take it. She couldn't help glancing at Mrs. Byrne then to see how Michael's mother was taking all of this, but found that her face was as coolly pleasant as a cameo carving. Mrs. Byrne returned Helena's gaze for only a moment.

Mrs. De Vries knew better than to go through a show of surprise. "Of course," she said understandingly. "Helena, too, can be quite elusive—but I'm sure you know how she lights up eventually, in the company of others."

"Indeed," Michael said, "I feel it's one of my great privileges to have encountered that light." Helena managed a smile.

Mrs. De Vries gave a musing "hmm" of agreement, set down her fork, and dabbed at her mouth with her napkin, having finished her portion of duck. Helena, meanwhile, had reduced hers by perhaps a quarter of an inch.

When her mother went on, her tone had intensified by a degree. She would never have been mistaken for anything but polite, but it was clear that she was coming to a point. "To pursue the topic of social engagements further... Mr. Byrne, Mrs. Byrne: you'll forgive me if I grow rather personal. I must confess now to a great, but I think natural, trepidation, on the part of my family, at the possibility of our youngest child departing us to form an alliance in a part of the country with which we've had little acquaintance—to our own discredit, I should add. What I would like to seek is reassurance. Re-assurance that, if we *were* to form an alliance, you would do everything within your power to ensure that Helena would have all the support she would need to form suitable social attachments in her... new home." The pause before her last words could have indicated an excess of maternal emotion—or the faintest shading of skepticism.

Mrs. Byrne stirred, now, and formed an expression of mild surprise. "Mrs. De Vries, your concern is appropriate, and touching. Yet I must remind you that Miss De Vries has been here for three months, under the chaperonage of her—

as Michael said—charming aunt. And of course she's graced more and more of our own occasions with her presence in the past month. She has had ample opportunity to be introduced to society here, and I assure you she's already spoken of with great admiration for her cultivation and beauty."

Helena felt a flare of ill temper at being discussed as if she were a greyhound or a show pony, but at this point, irritation was an almost pleasurable distraction from her worry for Michael. She stole a glance at him, but he was watching her mother evenly.

"Your reminder is well-taken," Mrs. De Vries conceded, "and I'm pleased to hear how my daughter has upheld her reputation. But I'm afraid I must continue to press the point. When I say 'suitable social attachments,' I mean to encompass attachments with—the wife *and* the husband. That is, I would like to form a better picture of what it might look like for Helena to make her entry into society here *as the wife of Mr. Byrne.*" A pause. "Mr. Byrne, I know I speak very plainly now, but you must admit that your situation is unusual. Is it at all fair for me to say that, until very recently, you have lived in seclusion?"

"It is fair," was all Michael said. His head was drooping forward slightly, but still his gaze on Helena's mother was unbroken.

Mrs. De Vries nodded. "And so it is also fair to say that a marriage would, moreover, represent your *own* entry into society here."

Michael hesitated. "That is also fair," he said.

Mrs. Byrne leaned forward stiffly, looking as if she wished to stop Michael from speaking further, her own lips parting to speak. But when Michael didn't acknowledge her movement, she closed her mouth and sat back slowly.

"And how," Mrs. De Vries inquired, "do you envision that that will proceed?" Her expression was one of pleasant interest.

Helena felt frozen, cold to her lips. She was mortified that her mother was conducting such a conversation over dinner and in front of the servants. Karl's face was as stoic as ever, but she could see tension in the set of his jaw, the subtle compression of his lips. She sent him a silent, desperate apology for exposing his master to this.

She knew what her mother was doing. *This is already more than enough,* her mother was saying. It was more than enough that she had interrupted her own plans, dashed across the entire country, and agreed to consider the suit of a preposterously unsuitable man over dinner. She had played her part with more than due courtesy, but now she must have the satisfaction of straight answers.

Helena could hear all her mother's unvoiced questions: *How do you propose to be taken seriously in public life when everybody understands that an infirm body means an infirm mind? How would you preside over a dinner when you cannot even hold your own knife? Have you ever even been in a restaurant, a theater, a streetcar?*

And, above all: *What would people think of my daughter, if she were to be known as the wife of a person like you?*

Helena looked at Michael's exhausted eyes, his sagging head; she could tell from the way that his body was leaning that his legs were pushing him to one side, unbalancing his seat. She wished she could take all of her own strength and pour it into his body.

The only thing that kept her from panic was something that she had told Michael again and again: if her mother came to California, it meant that *there was an opening*. Otherwise, Mrs. De Vries would simply never have come. She and Helena's father would have sent a letter demanding that Helena give up her attachment and return home at once, or else face disownment.

Could it be that some fraction of Mrs. De Vries *wanted* to be convinced that her daughter's courtship was possible? Was she curious to know how it might be achieved?

The only sound in the room was the ticking of the ormolu clock on the mantelpiece.

Mrs. De Vries and Michael were watching each other steadily. Michael's brows were drawn together with strain, and his head wavered on his neck, yet his expression looked measured, assessing.

He licked his lips and said finally, "Mrs. De Vries, I wish I could hand you an exact program of social appearances and conversational strategics that would result in my acceptance into society by a given date. But you know as well as I do that there's no forcing outcomes among people.

"What I can tell you is that—any of my efforts to live in the world will require support, and patience. I know that in hoping for you to be here tonight, I have already asked a great deal of you. But... rather than offering an immediate answer to your question, I must ask for one more thing from you, and that is... a little time. Five days. Maybe a week. Just a little time to get to know me, to spend time with me, to decide whether you feel you can trust me with... your daughter's reputation, your daughter's *happiness*." His voice was growing rough with emotion. "To decide whether you could ever imagine standing by me as... a member of your family.

"You can say 'no' now, or you can say 'no' in a few days. I must respect your decision at any point, because moving forward... would require your support. *We* would require your support." And he looked, for the first time in several minutes, straight at Helena. The heat in his eyes touched her.

He turned his gaze back to her mother. "If you decide tonight that you're willing to give me time..." His head suddenly dropped to his chest, cutting off his speech. He lifted it again; his expression had not changed. His eyes were bright and fierce with conviction. "If you and your husband were to consider embracing... a bond between Miss De Vries and me, I can promise you now that for the remainder of my life, I would never stop trying to honor her intelligence, her grace, her kindness, her beauty of spirit. Your daughter is a remarkable woman. With her friendship, she has already given me more than I can describe. It would be my privilege to be considered as anything close to her equal... in marriage. It would be my life's work."

The ticking of the clock reasserted its hold on the room. Mrs. De Vries lowered her eyes from Michael's; she looked to one side, with an uncertain twist to her lips. She looked bitter, or troubled.

When she finally spoke, her expression was resolute, almost stern. She placed each word as carefully as if she were setting down a line of stones. "Mr. Byrne. You speak very beautifully. And there's the wisdom of simplicity in what you say. Time *is* the most meaningful thing you could ask for. Yes, I will give you time. And I offer my sincere apology to both you and your mother for disrupting the evening in this way. It has been... a confusing time since we received your letters. Confusing, and difficult. I am... doing my best to understand, and to decide the best course of action for my family." Her gaze this time took in Helena.

"Your apology and your generosity are gratefully accepted," Mrs. Byrne put in smoothly. "And whatever else may happen, we are thankful for your company tonight." There may have been the faintest sheen of sweat on her ivory forehead.

With that, the room came unfrozen, as if in a fairy tale where servants and courtiers sprang back to life from an enchanted sleep. The salad course was brought in; napkins were shaken out and smoothed again; throats were cleared and seats adjusted. Helena exhaled and unclenched her hands from where she had knotted them together in her lap.

Her eyes sought Michael's; he gave her a faint, weary smile.

* * *

The remainder of the dinner was awkward, carried along

by a kind of effortful goodwill—but not unbearable. The relief from the tension and artificiality of the first half of the evening was so great that Helena was incredulous; she felt as if she had woken up in sweat-soaked sheets to find that a fever had broken. Several times, Michael even made Mrs. De Vries laugh; she looked less startled with each subsequent time that it happened.

Afterwards, as Helena and Mrs. De Vries were escorted out, the two mothers walked ahead, speaking quietly, so that Helena could contrive to linger behind with Michael. When their mothers disappeared around a turn in the corridor, she turned, putting out a hand to stop Karl pushing his chair, and flung her arms around Michael's neck. She kissed his cheek and whispered fiercely into his ear, "I'm so proud of you. You were marvelous."

He let out a long breath. "I'm going to need to sleep for twenty hours," he whispered back, "before I feel ready to take on your mother again."

Helena smiled. "I've felt that way before. And you'd better start sleeping now, because I think your mother is trying to convince mine that we should stay here for the rest of the week... Oh, Michael. Can we really do it all?"

He closed his eyes briefly. "Twenty hours. Ask me again after twenty hours."

She laughed a little and kissed his cheek again. "Sleep well, then, my love."

"Good night, Helena." He truly looked as if he were about to fall asleep in his chair, his eyes heavy-lidded, his hands lax in his lap, the fingers barely stirring. But his smile, as his eyes moved over her face, was content.

As she stood, she looked at Karl and felt a rush of gratitude for his steadiness, his discretion, his sensitivity. She put out a hand to touch his upper arm. "Thank you for being here tonight, Karl," she said.

He blinked. "I don't see how it could be otherwise, miss."

"I know—but you know what I mean. It's been a difficult evening. Thank you, and good night."

He inclined his head, holding it for a moment longer than usual.

Helena put a hand to her lips then, hesitating. She resisted the urge to kiss Michael once more, and hurried ahead to rejoin her mother.

* * *

Outside, Helena took a deep, grateful breath of the sweetly resinous California air. Insects chorused, and the sky was still suffused with the transparent blue glow of the long twilight. Helena and her mother stood above the semicircular drive, which curved along a shadowy mass of live oak trees, their sinuous shapes raw and vital.

Aunt Delia had lent her car and driver, Robert, to Mrs. De Vries for the evening, but Helena's mother held up a hand to him now to let him know that he should wait another minute for them. He tipped his cap and settled back into his seat.

Mrs. De Vries turned to face her daughter, looking at her searchingly in the low light. Helena tried not to glance away.

Their reunion before the dinner had been brief and brittle, as Mrs. De Vries had been rightfully offended by Helena's failure to meet her at the hotel. This was now her first real moment alone with her mother since she had departed for the West Coast. Looking at her mother, Helena realized with a pang that she had grown visibly older in the past three months—or perhaps Helena simply hadn't noticed it before. The streaks of silver in her dark hair had broadened, and even in the dusk light, her skin looked thinner, more fragile.

After Helena had sent home her letter about Michael, the reality of her behavior towards her parents had struck her. She had departed across the country, barely sent word home other than perfunctory reports concerning Aunt Delia's museum, and then suddenly reemerged with an astonishing, perturbing announcement. She clasped her hands together nervously now, overcome with a rush of guilt.

"I wish you had told me something sooner, Helena," her mother said. Her voice was soft, yet firm: a surprisingly gentle reproof.

Helena didn't want to stammer childishly, so she collected her thoughts before responding. "I didn't know my own mind for a long time, nor what might be possible. I wrote to you and Father truly as soon as I thought that there was something... I could fairly share."

Her mother sighed. "I suppose I can see how that would happen. Oh, you do like to bring us novel difficulties, Helena.

There, don't look so wounded. You can't imagine the commotion when we received your letters."

"I can, actually," Helena said, having inspired something like it once before.

"Well, then, imagine it tenfold. Your father asked, in all seriousness, if there were any nunneries left in America." Mrs. De Vries pushed out an explosive sigh of exasperation and flung up her hands. "When I set out on the train, I was ready to swoop down and declare that I was done being the kind of mother who attempts to understand her children's minds."

"And now...?" Helena pressed, sensing an opening.

Mrs. De Vries gave her a long look. "Despite all of my intentions otherwise... I can understand why you care for him so much," she said very softly.

Helena covered her mouth with her hand, blinking hard. "Thank you," she whispered, "for saying so."

"He seems... frail, though. Are you *entirely* sure... Can he really...?"

Helena watched her mother, whose effort to hold back a flood of objections and questions was clear, and almost physical.

"He was tired, tonight," Helena replied with deliberation. "He can look quite different from day to day. But he's stronger than you might think."

Her mother gave her a dry look. "I take your meaning. Well, I did promise him time. I promised you both time. So I shall do my best to watch, and understand. But, Helena..." A warning note had entered her voice. "One more word from me, and then we can spend the drive in blessed silence, and you shall nestle your head on my shoulder so I can pretend you're my docile lambkin and not the most confounding child."

Helena bit her lip, smiling. "Yes, Mother?"

"You don't need me to tell you that this will all be very difficult indeed. But what strikes me is that... despite your occasional forays into melodrama, you have rarely liked to take the lead. Your preference is to make things happen behind the scenes. Is that right?"

"It is," Helena admitted.

"Whatever happens, wherever you go, if you persist in this course... it will be exceedingly difficult for Mr. Byrne to be taken seriously. It would *oblige* you to take the lead. Many women would find that exhausting. Perhaps, eventually, disappointing. It often happens, you know, that a wife comes to resent her husband—or the other way round—because something about him obliges her to act against her disposition." Her mother watched her, askance.

Helena thought of Aunt Delia cajoling men to stand in for her so that she could buy the art she liked at auction. She thought how silly it all was, how exhaustingly circuitous, for there to be so many rules about who could do what and when. She thought of her first night with Michael, when, despite all her misgivings, she had pushed matters forward, and forward again, and beauty had come of it.

All of a sudden, she felt her fatigue weighing her down.

She said carelessly, "Maybe I shall learn to like it. Maybe I've already learned to like it."

Her mother examined her for a moment longer before turning to signal to Robert. "Well, we'll see," she said neutrally.

Helena reached out for her mother, then, wrapping both her arms around her.

But as Robert pulled the car up, her mother burst out once more, with a kind of despairing humor: "But *Helena*—he has a twin brother!"

Helena had to laugh. "Oh, Mother. There was never any choice between the two."

* * *

Ten months later, Mr. and Mrs. Michael Byrne departed New York by steamer for Paris, there to begin their honeymoon.

Acknowledgements

Many, many thanks to Lucy May Lennox and K. S. for their thoughtful feedback on this story.

I would also like to acknowledge the inspirations I drew upon, however obliquely, for this work:

Books and films

The novels and short stories of F. Scott Fitzgerald (of course), particularly "Bernice Bobs Her Hair" (1920)

The Devil in the White City, by Eric Larson (2003)

There Will Be Blood, directed by Paul Thomas Anderson (2007)

Scholarship

"But Roosevelt Could Walk": Envisioning Disability in Germany and the United States. Article by Carol Poore in *Disability, Art, and Culture* (1998)

People and places

For Aunt Delia: Lady Ottoline Morrell (1873-1938) and Isabella Stewart Gardner (1840-1924)

For Aunt Delia's architect, Jane Montague: Julia Morgan (1872-1957)

The Isabella Stewart Gardner Museum and the Museum of Fine Arts in Boston, Massachusetts

The Cloisters Museum in New York

The Getty Villa in Los Angeles, California

Hearst Castle in San Simeon, California

The war that Delia and Helena allude to around Thessaloniki, Greece, is the Greco-Turkish War of 1919-1922.

www.ingramcontent.com/pod-product-compliance
Lightning Source LLC
Chambersburg PA
CBHW060455300726
48975CB00008B/2519